One Last Kill

– DESMOND MCGRATH –

Best wishes from Des

An environmentally friendly book printed and bound in England by
www.printondemand-worldwide.com

i

www.fast-print.net/store.php

One Last Kill
Copyright © Desmond McGrath 2011

All characters are fictional.
Any similarity to any actual person is purely coincidental.

ISBN 978-178035-205-3

First published 2011 by
FASTPRINT PUBLISHING
Peterborough, England.

Dedication

To my Dad Patrick, my two young brothers and my father in law. Phil, Ed and George. Sadly no longer with us.

Also in the Jack Reec series:

Private Execution

The Executioner

Desmond McGrath

Part One

Costa del Sol, Spain

Desmond McGrath

One

I was a desperately lonely man.

Desperate!

My wife and friends were gone.

Murdered.

I was being released from hospital, shot up but recovering from my wounds. I was going to go back to my farm a few miles south of Marbella in Southern Spain.

I would have much time to ponder on the mistakes I had made in my life. And there were many.

I was able to drive, and took my open-top Jaguar XK8 from Málaga along the most dangerous road in Spain, past Torremolinos,

Benalmadena Costa, Feungirola and Mijas, through Marbella and San Pedro de Alcantara to the peace and quiet of the countryside and wildlife on and around my farm on the Costa del Sol.

I crunched the Jaguar onto the gravel parking area adjacent to the bar and pool and sat in the warm midmorning sun reliving past happy memories.

I hadn't been here for over two months, and it showed. It had the look of an empty home on the market to be sold.

But it wasn't for sale.

I pulled myself with difficulty from the low seat of the convertible and strolled aimlessly around, gathering my thoughts and figuring out a plan to clean the place up again.

The pool was dirty and covered in floating leaves and miscellaneous debris. Some of it had sunk to the blue tiled bottom. The loungers were covered in thick dust. To a man in despair it all looked so hopelessly irretrievable.

And then, on a flurry of a breeze from the mountains off to the north, I was hit by the smell of the earth. My orchard of oranges, lemons and limes filled my nostrils with the overwhelming scent of the farm.

I was home. Home alone.

Desmond McGrath

Two

I had done it the easy way.

I called in the cleaners and property maintenance specialists who expertly prepared the thousands of homes for sale in Spain. Soon the place was like new again.

I was now relishing the total peace and quiet. I was alone and wanted to stay alone for a very long time.

Possibly forever.

The only people I saw or had contact with were the delivery people who brought me fresh food and drink.

I spent my days reading books, drinking, eating and building my strength up again, swimming and sunbathing in the early season sunshine.

In some strange way I was content in my sadness and loneliness.

The bullet wounds in each shoulder were mending well, but it was the one in my leg that caused me difficulty and seemed to ache constantly. It was the kind of pain that was not unbearable but seemed to be forever there, dragging me down.

I was lying by the pool with God knows how many beers inside me reading a James Patterson book and drifting into my daily state of inebriation, where for the thousandth time I trawled through the events that had shaped my life and brought me to the point that I was at.

This miserable existence... Millions in the bank, my own farm in Southern Spain, an open top Jaguar, as much food and drink as I wanted, and no need ever to work again for the rest of my life!

I was feeling sorry for myself.

But I had been out of hospital for six weeks now and had to move on.

Three

The price of gold was at an all-time high. And I had gold a plenty. A plane full of it. At today's prices, at least 10 million dollars.

My wounds were all but healed. But I needed to get fit. A few weeks regular training would see to that. I began gently and raised the game progressively. I was starting to feel good again.

And starting to look good again. I was six feet and half an inch, lean, tanned and just turned forty.

A handsome-looking bastard, I had always thought. Deep blue eyes, sharp features and a full head of hair.

A Falklands veteran and an expert salvage diver, I had lived life in the fast lane. Fast cars and beautiful women. My granddad always told me, 'Get the car first, son, and the women will follow.'

And granddad wasn't wrong. Cars, booze, women - I'd done the lot.

And by fuck I wasn't finished yet!

Jack was back.

Sorry. By the way, the name's Jack.

Jack Reec.

Four

The gold was in a sunken Lear Jet that had crashed into a Spanish lake high in the mountains. It was stolen gold from the infamous Brinks Mat robbery in the early eighties.

Sam Kennedy was flying to a new life with it when the plane crashed in a violent storm and lay undiscovered for over twenty years, until I found it by accident while diving illegally in the lake for pleasure.

The lake was forbidden to divers but that meant nothing to me. I find it hard to live by the rules; I never have and still never do.

I met Sam Kennedy for the first time twenty years after his death.

He didn't say a lot.

In fact he looked really pissed off.

His skeletal remains were still strapped in his seat and only held together by his rotting clothes. A fish had taken up residence in his head and nestled comfortably, watching me from his eye socket.

Miguel Lopez, Sam's pilot, was slumped over his controls and beginning to collapse into a pile of bones.

The richest two skeletons in all of Spain, I'd thought at the time.

All that gold...

And then I came along.

I only took one bar.

Just a sample.

But it was that small sample that was eventually to lead to the murder of my best friend Richard Bull.

One thing led to another, and I ended up building a gallows in my barn and holding a private execution.

I hanged the bastard.

But did it really make me feel better?

Yes, it fucking did.

A lot better.

So when a psychopathic killer called David Walker slaughtered my girlfriend I decided to slaughter him back.

Trouble was, I forgot to give David Walker the script. After hunting him down to Morocco he killed my two best friends, Jesús Alcantara, Spanish Special Forces, and Sebastian Aparicio, a Spanish policeman.

No mean feat.

And then, when he could easily have killed me, he shot me in both shoulders and one leg.

He spared my life so I could suffer some more.

Well, I was tired of suffering. I was going to get my life back again.

I was going to renew my acquaintance with Sam Kennedy.

And his gold.

I checked my list of friends.

Liam Dooly.

IRA enforcer.

Dooly had been sent to kill me. He didn't, and we became friends.

Weary of killing, he did one more.

The Last Hit.

A million euros.

And retirement back to the Auld Country.

Ireland.

Dublin.

I caught a plane.

Five

David Walker had a new identity.

And he hadn't killed for ages. The treatment seemed to be working. It cost a fortune, but money was no matter. He was independently rich, with 'old money'.

He had only been in love once. Once in all of his life. And here he was, thirty-six, rich and suavely handsome, but with no one he could call his own.

Her name had been Jane. A holiday rep he had met on his serial killing spree.

The sole survivor.

God, how lucky was she to have loved him.

And survived.

He thought about her often. Every day in fact.

He'd spared her!

Hadn't he?

Well, not really, he supposed.

She'd escaped.

And the fucking bastard bitch had tried to kill him into the bargain. Smashed him over the head with an onyx table lamp.

Still, he thought, she didn't know he was going to spare her.

She deserved the benefit of the doubt.

He decided to find her again. He knew she would be pining over him.

She'd never really get over him.

She deserved another chance.

Didn't she?

Six

The Pogues still rule in the Spotted Dog in Dublin.

'Dirty Old Town' still blasted out on the jukebox as fresh as the day they recorded it.

Fuck knows how long ago.

Dooly didn't care. It still sounded great.

The room a haze of blue smoke. No smoking ban here. I couldn't see him as I entered. I weaved my way to the bar. It was the accent that gave me away.

'A pint of Guinness, please,' I ordered, 'and an Irish whiskey while it's pouring.'

'Yer got the drink right, Brit,' smiled Maggie, 'just the wrong pub.'

'I don't think so, Maggie,' I grinned back at her.

'How'd yer know my name, Brit?' Maggie asked.

'I've heard enough about you,' I told her.

'And who would that be squealing?' she asked suspiciously.

'A scut named Dooly.'

The room quietened.

'You better watch who you're calling a scut, mister.'

'I'm dying of thirst here, Maggie, and you haven't even started to pour my drink.'

'Nor will I be, and if you know what's good for you, Brit, you'll get your arse out of here while you still have legs to drag it.'

'Maggie, Maggie, Maggie, for Jazus' sake, is that any way to be treating a man's best friend?'

Dooly threw his arms around me and slapped the wind out of my back.

'Holy Mary, Mother of God. As I live and breathe. Jack Reec!'

'Liam,' I cried, tearfully hugging him back.

'You murdering bastard!'

'The very same.'

'Liam ...' I started.

'I know, auld son.'

A tear from each eye tramlined down his cheeks.

'Maggie. Bushmills... a bottle. Let's give this man the best welcome in all Ireland.' The room erupted to the Pogues.

Seven

'So what is it, Jack?' Dooly asked as we pulled two old chairs from under a rough old wooden table and sat. He poured two fingers of Irish into a couple of tumblers as Maggie delivered two still clearing pints of Guinness.

'Sorry about earlier,' she apologised. 'How could I have known Liam had changed sides?'

'You can make it up to him later, Maggie,' Dooly said with a wink.

'Dream on, old man!'

Dooly had forgotten that Maggie was still only twenty.

'Liam,' I scolded, 'don't be too hard on the girl. She hasn't yet developed a taste for vintage wine. But she will.'

'To be sure, to be sure,' he boomed, as he slapped her arse and the room erupted.

'I suppose a taste wouldn't hurt,' Maggie cried good-naturedly as the Pogues burst into 'Dirty Old Town' for the umpteenth time.

'Up the arse,' screamed Dooly. 'Up the arse!' screamed the room. I was dreading the hangover.

Eight

'**S**o you want to go after the gold, auld son,' said Dooly. 'I thought you were saving it for your pension.'

'I was. But the price of gold is going through the roof daily and I need something to do,' I told him.

'Sure enough, auld son. I suppose salvaging 10 million dollars in gold is as good a way as any to relieve the boredom,' Dooly remarked as he downed a Bushmills.

'I've set my heart on an ocean-going cruiser,' I confessed, 'and that takes dough! Serious dough. Not to mention the costs of running it.'

'I hear what you're saying, auld son.'

'And then there's the Lamborghini.'

'A fucking Lamborghini?'

'You bet.'

'Is it a crisis you're having, auld son?' Dooly asked incredulously. "'Cause it sounds like it to me.'

'Well, I'm not sure about a crisis,' I told him. 'I've had enough of those for sure. But if I'm having another one I want to make sure it's a good one for a change.'

Dooly started building the makings of a cigarette. He licked the paper and rolled it between his fingers and tapped it on the table at both ends.

He lit it and drawled thoughtfully. 'And where do I come in to all this?'

'You're the only friend I have left,' I told him honestly. 'All the rest are dead. You'll have to do.'

A chuckle crept from Dooly's lips as he sat back in his chair. 'Youse can stuff the boat, Jack, but I could use a Lamborghini.'

'That's the deal then, Liam,' I declared. 'A Lamborghini.'

Nine

When the door opened at Malaga the warm dusty air met my face and washed over me. I swallowed it wholesomely, as did Dooly.

"Tis good to be back, Jack,' was all he said.

'Yes,' I replied simply.

We collected the XK8 from the airport car park and dropped the hood.

We sped the miles to the farm.

"Tis a lonely auld place, Jack,' Dooly sighed, 'without them.'

'For sure it is, Liam,' I sighed back.

He was referring to Barbara, my murdered girlfriend and her dead avengers, Sebastian

27

Aparicio and Jesus Alcantara.

'But they are gone,' I said, 'and we have to move on. We have both seen much death in our lifetime and we both know that it can't be dwelt upon. The grieving is over. We'll never forget them but life has to go on.'

The afternoon was turning to dusk. A few wild birds were calling to their partners to return for the night. The shadows spread across the garden and peace and tranquillity settled over the land. Out here in the Spanish countryside the dusk quickly descended into the darkness of the night.

I lit the pool area and we lazed back in our loungers with beers. We both sucked deeply on the warm night air.

'Jack, I'm fucking starving,' Dooly howled, raising his San Miguel to his mouth. 'Is there any fucking food?'

So I fired up the barbecue and lumped on two T-bones. I popped the cork on a bottle of Cava Aristel and, after tasting it from the bottle, I poured two glasses.

We need music.

'The Pogues,' howled Dooly.

'Fuck the Pogues!' I laughed. 'This is Spain.'

Turning up the volume, Ricky Martin blasted out 'Livin' La Vida Loca.

We finished the T-bones and opened more Aristel.

'I love you, Jack, but this is a piss poor party. Where are the fucking girls?'

I had to agree.

But I'd had no other woman since Barbara. A lifetime ago.

I said so.

'What did we just say, Jack?'

'Life goes on,' I replied.

He was right.

I made a call.

Her warm sultry voice seemed to float out of the receiver, washing down my neck and tickling my back. It was Horny Formore's voice on the answering machine. If ever I get knocked down by a bus and go into a coma, play me tapes of Horny Formore's voice. I'll either wake up or die happy.

I told her to pick up if she was there.

She did.

We fixed a price and she was invited to the party.

With a friend.

Wait for it: Delicious Fantastico.

For fuck's sake!

Ten

They arrived in a top-down red Ferrari. Horny Formore and Delicious Fantastico. I was sure they could easily afford it!

Horny opened the door and a leg the length of an anaconda slithered from it. She raised herself out and I saw a lash of red hair cascading down to sun-browned shoulders. She had a wide mouth with dazzling white perfect teeth. Then my eyes drifted to breasts thrusting to get out of a backless white dress that stuck to her waist and hips and ended above the most perfect calves I've ever seen. She was an absolute angel.

Delicious Fantastico was like a dark chocolate ice cream melting and begging to be licked. She demanded to be tasted. Long and slender, she oozed Spanish aristocracy and sheer class. She shook her long black wavy hair. It glistened in the moonlight. She held her handbag like a catwalk model, any one of which she could easily outshine. Her huge brown eyes battled with her astonishing mouth and teeth for attention. Her knee-length clinging red dress was split up the thigh, demanding to be noticed.

We noticed.

'Well, shall we all relax?' I greeted them. 'I'm Jack, this is Liam. There is no rush, let's all have a good time. I want no ceremony. This is a party. We are all friends. There is no rush. Stay for the night and breakfast.'

The ice was melted and the girls were great company.

Eleven

A few wisps of grey cloud drifted like cigar smoke across the dark night sky and occasionally partially faded the moon. The air was warm that evening, with a soft breeze coming from the sea, carrying a hint of tangy salt on it. It strayed through the citrus grove collecting the scent of oranges, lemons and limes. Along with the taste of the earth and dry leaves it heightened our senses to the beauty all around us.

'It is the most wonderful place you have here, Jack,' Delicious Fantastico told me, as she leaned back in her lounger and drank cava, still fizzing in the flute I had just poured her.

I held my glass in both hands in my lap, stretching slightly, a little tired. 'It seems a lonely place these days,' I said. I'd already told her of the tragedies that had overtaken me.

33

'Yes Jack, but you must begin to live again,' she sighed, reaching across to gently feel my hands.

'I'm trying. But it's not easy.'

'Let me help you, Jack,' she whispered seductively. 'After all, that is what you are paying me for. Enjoy.'

Delicious Fantastico was without doubt one of the most beautiful women I had ever seen, let alone shagged. She eased the glass from my hands as she put hers down and raised her long slender body to her feet.

'The pool is heated, Jack?' she asked.

'Of course,' I said, 'it always is at night.'

'Can we swim, then?'

'For sure,' I said.

Delicious slipped a hand behind her back, and the knee-length clinging red dress split to the thigh fell to the ground.

She was totally naked without it.

I stared at her and felt the excitement rushing through me like hot lava bursting up a volcano to the lip of the crater.

She wore no body hair and was as smooth as

smoked glass. She stepped across my outstretched legs and threw back her hair.

'Fill my glass please, Jack.'

I filled it for her, and she leaned her head back to drink. Arching her back slightly she let the sizzling cava pour down her chin and neck through the valley of her mountainous breasts, past her belly button and down over her vagina.

'Oh God, Jack, I'm so sorry. I've spilled it. Don't waste it!'

I didn't. Holding the bottle up to my mouth I swallowed greedily and when it washed back I thrust my mouth between her legs ravenously. As I worked my tongue into her she took the bottle from me and poured more cava over my face and into her now open space.

I held her firm buttocks and pulled her further into my face. I was throbbing now. She cupped my face in both hands and squatted down. She took some cava in her mouth and kissed me with passion as we both swallowed together. She rose slowly to her feet, bringing me up with her. She cupped both thumbs inside my shorts and slid them down. Something inside them was straining to get out.

The band of my shorts released it and it sprang back up positively pulsing.

'How do you want it, Jack?'

'Any way it comes.'

'Delicious or Fantastico?' she asked, and howled with laughter.

I guessed she'd cracked that joke before.

'In the pool.'

I sucked on her beautiful Spanish lips, newly filled with cava.

'Delicious!' I cried.

Bottle and all, we fell backwards into the pool.

'Fantastico!' she screamed.

I was rampant now. I couldn't wait any longer. I pushed her back to the wall and opened her wide with my fingers. I pushed inside her and found my rhythm. Like a flamenco beat, it got faster and faster and faster. Then with a scream of ecstasy that sent two sleeping birds flapping from the trees, I collapsed my weight on to her.

'Better now?' she asked me tenderly.

I just nodded. 'You bet.'

It was then that I heard Dooly shouting and

cheering with laughter. Standing by the pool with his arm around the waist of Horny Formore he said, 'Jesus, Jack, that's going to be a hard act to follow.'

'Well, you'd better get started, Dooly auld son,' mimicked Horny Formore. I nearly died of embarrassment. I had completely forgotten they were there. But I wasn't really bothered.

That night I had fulfilled a lifetime ambition and reached the plateau of ultimate pleasure. Now is all we get.

Desmond McGrath

Twelve

Breakfast was a grand affair. We ate around the pool.

I had spent the whole night comfortably in the arms of Delicious and completely forgot that she was a hooker. She was *fantastic*, after all.

And it was only a job.

I once had a job.

Killing people!

What was worse?

Who was I to judge?

Liam Dooly and Horny Formore had never stopped laughing from the time they met.

Nobody made judgements.

Horny was a 'madam' hooker and good at it.

Dooly was an IRA gunman and hit man.

Who cared?

We all had to make a living. And no one of us was qualified to make judgements.

And none of us wanted to.

An odd lot, just thrown together by circumstances.

But as it would turn out, forever to be friends.

And look out for each other.

My doctor, Doctor Susan, would never have approved. But tough shit.

It was buck's fizz for breakfast on the first day of my new life, not warm milk.

Horny Formore and I compared the merits of our cars. She preferred the Ferrari. I saw its plus points but argued for the Jaguar XKS on the grounds that it had four seats.

She didn't need four seats, and countered by asking how many times did I need four seats. I argued, if I didn't need four seats I'd rather have a Lamborghini.

She said, 'In that case, have a fucking Lamborghini.'

'OK then. I'll have a fucking Lamborghini.'

'So what the fuck do I care!'

'Am I paying for you or what?' I demanded.

'You're paying me to get fucked,' she countered, 'not to tell me what car to drive.'

Exasperated, I said, 'Just stick it up your arse, will you.' 'You have to pay extra for that!' she cried. We both fell about laughing.

Desmond McGrath

Thirteen

'Jack, you throw a fucking great party,' Dooly said, more of a statement.

'I know,' I said smugly.

'That Horny's some fucking bitch.'

'I know.'

'Where did you find her?'

'Round about.'

'Don't fuck with me, Jack.'

'So what's it got to do with you?' I asked him. 'You didn't pay for her.'

'I like her, Jack.'

'She's just a whore.'

'And I'm a killer.'

'So?'

'It's a fucking job, for Christ's sake.'

'So?'

'So. I'd like to see her again.'

'And?'

'And! What the fuck's it got to do with you?'

'I paid her.'

'I'll give you the fucking money.'

'OK.'

'And are youse trying to tell me you don't want to see the fucking ice cream.'

'Yes,' I said, 'but it's none of your fucking business, because I paid for her too!'

'Bollocks, Jack.'

I held both hands in the air. 'Liam, I'm playing. I know what you're saying. We're all professionals of one sort or another and it would be great to see it all work out. But for now let's keep to the business in hand. The gold. That's what we have got to focus on. The girls are a great diversion but let's not get carried away. They're working girls and we can have them any time we want. They're on the other end of the phone.'

'As ever, you're right, to be sure. The gold it is, then. So what's the plan?'

Desmond McGrath

Fourteen

Dooly sat relaxing in a lounger by the pool with a bottle of San Miguel in one hand and a half-smoked White Owl New Yorker in the other. His thoughts, I'm sure, were the same as mine. He was reliving his night of ecstasy with Horny Formore.

My whole body was still tingling from the most erotic experience of my life. Immersed in a dreamy haze, I forked over steaks on the sizzling, smoking barbecue with the sun gently warming my almost black back.

Life was feeling good again. An arrowhead of wild geese squawked loudly overhead as they flew in perfect formation away to the freedom of somewhere new. They flapped their wings easily and grew smaller towards the distant horizon.

A light breeze moved the leaves on the trees

around my house and I sighed deeply with a touch of sadness and loneliness as I swigged from the neck of my beer.

Charcoal, searing beef and cigar smoke mingled with the smell of the beer in my nose. The steaks were done.

I skewered them roughly onto plates and shouted, 'Dooly!'

We sat at the bar on stools with fresh bottles and chewed as we spoke. The steaks were delicious, with far more salt and pepper than was healthy.

But then again, we didn't really do a lot that was healthy.

'I don't know much about this diving crack,' Dooly confessed. 'How long would it take to recover the gold? And what would you need?'

'All I would need is the diving gear I already have,' I told him. 'But we can't just go there and spend a week recovering it in broad daylight.'

'How so?'

'The gold is in the cargo hold of a Lear Jet. It's on the bottom of a lake in the hills above Málaga. It's a busy tourist destination in season, and this is season. There are coaches arriving and departing all day. Diving is not allowed. We would have to get there at daylight in the morning and be gone before they open the place up.

'Sounds simple enough, auld son,' Dooly said chewing steak and washing it down with beer. 'So what's the problem?'

'The jet is out on the far side of the lake in about a hundred feet. We can't risk using a boat, so I have to swim from the shore underwater and back. I can only bring one bar at a time. So I reckon the most we could do is two trips a morning.'

'How many bars do you reckon there are?' asked Dooly.

'About fifty or sixty, I'd say. Couldn't count them properly. They're spilled about all over the place.'

'Jesus, auld son,' Dooly whistled through his teeth. 'That's a lot of fucking gold.'

'At the time, I figured about 5 million quid. But at today's prices, ten.' 'Jesus, Mary and Joseph!. 10 million fucking quid!'

Desmond McGrath

Fifteen

The Serious Crimes Squad had never given up completely on the Brinks Mat gold. The case was still open.

They knew that one solitary bar had surfaced on the Costa del Sol and been linked in some way to two completely differing people.

Mak 'the Knife', as he was nicknamed because of his preference to murder with a blade, had disappeared off the face of the planet.

Underworld sources in Spain and local rumour had it that he was murdered, execution-style.

But not by shooting.

By hanging.

Hanged by the second man linked to the gold: Jack Reec.

No amount of investigation, no matter how thorough, could link Reec to the robbery.

A decorated Falklands veteran and expert scuba-diver with no criminal record, he was clean.

But it had been Reec who took the gold ingot to a jeweller in Torremolinos to be valued. It was this that kicked off a whole chain of events.

It was soon after that that Reec's best friend, Richard Bull, was murdered.

Stabbed.

It was soon after that that Mak the Knife's bar was blown up.

Then his car was blown up.

A boat full of drugs he was expecting was blown up.

Then his house was blown up.

And for all the Serious Crimes Squad knew, Mak the Knife was blown up too!

Because they never fucking saw or heard of him again.

Nor his bird.

Nor his gang.

All blown up?

Who knows?

But Jack Reec wasn't blown up. And with no visible source of income was living the life of a millionaire just south of Marbella.

So with the credit crunch beginning to bite into the already low wages of a policeman with extravagant tastes, Colin Simpkins had been doing a little free time research into Jack Reec.

With a little help from some friends, of course.

And what had he found out?

Links with the IRA.

Links with the Spanish Police.

Links with ETA, the Basque separatist organisation based in Spain.

All of whom lately had sustained fatal casualties while with Jack Reec.

Reec himself had sustained serious wounds and was only now, after several months, recovering.

Who was Reec?

And why had he flown to the Emerald Isle and returned to his farm with one of the most notorious IRA gunmen in all Ireland?

Liam Dooly.

The man who Intelligence knew had been responsible for the assassination of Danny 'Wonder Boy' McReynolds, the Manchester United captain, on the pitch at Villa Park... and ultimately his traitorous father, Sean McReynolds.

There had to be a connection in all of this. And Colin Simpkins was going to find it.

Sixteen

Colin Simpkins had seriously damaged his back in the line of duty while arresting a man far heavier than him who had fallen heavily on top of him on a concrete pavement.

He was on indefinite, fully paid, sick leave. The doctors had recommended complete rest and, if possible, some sun on his back in a warm climate.

As he climbed down the steps of the plane at Málaga Airport the hot air hit him, almost pushing him back.

He collected his bag and passed quickly through the airport to a waiting taxi that took him speedily the few miles to Torremolinos. Where the whole story of the gold had started. According to what he had been told, anyway.

Not bad looking, and six feet tall with short black hair and deep steel blue eyes, Colin Simpkins always had a sly, mischievous smile for the ladies.

In fact Simpkins considered himself to be quite a ladies' man.

The ladies, however, saw Colin Simpkins as a sleazebag. In fact he had even once been called a slimeball.

Sleazebag or slimeball? Take your pick.

Choosing the anonymity of a large hotel, Simpkins had booked a room at the Hotel Sol Principe. It was a four-star, good quality hotel, with all the facilities, and overlooked the beach. With 600 rooms it was mainly a package holiday hotel, which to Colin Simpkins meant that there had to be a good chance of pulling.

The standard room was brightly furnished in orange. It would sleep three so it was more than big enough for one.

And hopefully sometimes two.

It was mid-afternoon and he decided to visit the pool bar. He found an empty table. Immediately a waiter appeared and took his order for a large beer. He felt slightly overdressed in long trousers and short-sleeved shirt, but he hadn't bothered to change in his haste for a drink.

No matter. He leaned back in his chair and scanned the poolside. Taking a long, long drink, he sighed deeply and closed his eyes a few seconds for a little tranquillity. As he opened them slowly he feasted on the abundant variety of tits.

Big tits, small tits, all kinds of tits. Tits galore.

Desmond McGrath

Seventeen

Having decided that Jane deserved another chance, he set out to find her. He guessed where she'd be. At the hotel where she was a holiday rep: Hotel Parador Nacional de la Arruzafa in Córdoba.

In his hired Mercedes SLK200 he drove, top down, at his own leisurely pace, drinking in the beauty of the countryside. He hadn't spent a great deal of time in the area when he had met Jane there, but erring on the side of caution, he had changed his appearance slightly.

With his hair longer and a small neat moustache, he was sure that nobody would recognise the psychopathic serial killer who savagely mutilated the bodies of his victims.

Only Jane, he hoped. Sweet Jane. Sole survivor Jane.

After reaching the hotel, he checked in and took his small travel bag to the room. Then, as he had done before, he took himself to the poolside bar and a bottle of his favourite cava, Freixenet. It came to him beautifully presented in an ice bucket with a crisp towel over the top. The waiter set down two Freixenet flutes and filled just one, as David Walker had asked.

He supped at the fizzy wine and recalled Jane to memory. A real looker: blond, slim and tanned, with a warm, friendly smile.

'Are you fucking crazy?' Jane shouted, half in panic. 'What the fuck are you doing here?' She sat down quickly beside him, eyes darting everywhere.

'I had to see you,' Came the blunt reply

'You stupid fucking cunt! If anyone ever sees you, you'll be locked up for the rest of your life.'

'Jane, Jane, be calm. It's all right,' he tried to assure her. 'Nobody even knows I'm in Spain.'

'You're mad.'

'I'm not. I'm not. Listen to me. I have a new name. A new identity. I've changed my appearance,' he reasoned.

'I knew you straight away,' Jane argued, 'the moment I saw you.'

'Yes but you love me.'

'Love you!' Jane exclaimed. 'You're an insane murderer.'

'What's that got to do with anything?' David Walker laughed, all his boyish charm shining through.

'You what?'

'Jane, you don't believe all of that, surely?' he asked her sincerely.

'David,' she said seriously, 'I saw you shoot two Spanish policemen with my own eyes.'

'They were trying to kill me, Jane,' he reasoned. 'You know that. You saw it. You were there, for God's sake.'

'I know I was fucking there! You scared the shit out of me.'

'Then you knew I had to do it.'

'And what about the others?'

'What others?'

'Jack Reec and his two friends.'

'The ones who were hunting me down like a dog. The bastards who accused me of killing all those women. The fuckers who accused me of killing you! But you're not fucking dead, are you?' He stared into her eyes.

'These fuckers? Yes, I killed them. Before they killed me... And while we're on the subject, I didn't kill Reec. The biggest murdering bastard of them all.'

'Why?'

'Because he was no longer a threat to me! That's why. Because I only kill when I have to. And if you don't believe that, then you might as well fuck off now.'

'Finished?' she asked.

'Yes.'

'Then pour me a drink. Cunt!'

Eighteen

We planned a recce to the lake. Dooly wanted to see it anyway.

I'd checked and serviced all my diving gear and figured out what needed to be figured out which wasn't much, and decided on a day to make the trip.

We started early in the morning. I'd cleaned and polished the open-top Jaguar for the trip. We cruised through the countryside, wind in our hair, passing orange groves, lemon groves, lime groves and everything else, the smells changing constantly as we approached the more barren hills.

Eventually we coasted into a large dirt car park and stopped beyond the end of a line of parked coaches.

'Tis a fine place Jack,' said Dooly, removing his sunglasses. 'I can see what it is that captured your heart.'

'I have some fine memories of the place,' I told him. 'Some good, some bad.'

'To be sure, auld son.'

'It was here I shot the head off a dirty lying bastard, Patsy Cronin, with a pump-action shotgun.'

'Not me auld friend Patsy! And him a God fearin man. Shame on you, Jack. 'Tis a pagan you are!'

I had a chuckle at the memory. Not that it was really funny. But I could still see the dirty double-crossing bastard's head disintegrate in a misty pink and grey spray.

'Have you any more happy memories to share with me, Jack?' Dooly asked.

'To be sure, to be sure,' I mimicked.

We laughed at that and began our climb up a rocky dirt path to the bar-restaurant that overlooked the lake. It was almost lunchtime and the smells of garlic, charcoal, sardines, steak and chops mingled with the smoke. We picked up two large beers on our way to the table.

Sitting in the shade looking out and down over the lake, we watched the tourists in their long flat rowing boats splashing each other with the sole intention of getting soaked. The surrounding rock face supported little vegetation as it held captive the smooth, still water that dazzled in the sun.

Splashing their oars onto the water, the name of the game for the tourists was to soak the other guy as much as they could. People fell overboard and climbed back in, little realising that they were playing above a crashed jet, two skeletons and £10 million in gold.

Desmond McGrath

Nineteen

Colin Simpkins 'El Slimeball' was proving true to his reputation. Having singled out a likely target, he began in his mind rehearsing his bullshit.

The pretty woman was short, five one maybe, slim, dark-haired with a narrow waist and breasts that were large and firm.

The kids were obviously driving her nuts. It seemed to come as an enormous relief when the hotel's children's representative took them off her hands to the 'Kiddies Club'.

A few hours of peace.

She flopped at the table next to El Slimeball. A gin and tonic arrived simultaneously.

'*Gracias*, Pedro,' the young woman smiled.

'*De nada, señora,*' the handsome waiter replied. 'It is that time, *sí?*'

'*Sí,*' she said, 'my time.'

Colin Simpkins spread his mouth in his sly, mischievous smile as he raised his glass in a toast, 'To a few hours of heavenly peace and quiet.'

'I'll certainly drink to that,' the pretty brunette laughed.

'Mind if I join you? I'm not armed,' El Slimeball joked.

'Not yet, anyway,' the pretty brunette returned with an equally sly smile.

Simpkins moved across the short gap to her table and to the left of her. He introduced himself directly to her breasts. 'I'm Colin, pleased to meet you.'

'Tiffany,' she replied offering her hand in a brief shake. 'Tiffany Pissed Off.'

'That's an unusual name,' El Slimeball laughed. 'I like it.'

'Just arrived?' Tiffany Pissed Off asked.

'Less than an hour ago.'

'Then you get lucky quick.'

'How so?'

'I need a good fucking. And I need it now.'

'Do we have time for another drink?'

'I guess so.'

'Your place or mine?'

'You alone?'

'Yes.'

'Yours then.'

Pissed Off and Slimeball had a couple more gin and tonics to get to know each other better, then left separately and arrived together at Slimeball's room, Slimeball with a bottle of wine and two glasses.

The house wine. No need for extravagance on this girl. Closing the door behind them, they stripped off naked.

'No biting, scratching or marking,' Pissed Off told him.

Slimeball drank a third of the wine from the bottle and said, 'You got it.'

Putting down the bottle, they fell onto the bed.

Filthy, dirty sex was what they both wanted and there was no holding back. Slimeball's manhood was hard and ample. Pissed Off mounted it like a jockey on a horse. He thrust and she pushed. Lowering her head to his mouth, she kissed him passionately with a slobbering, probing tongue. Holding her bottom he pulled her even deeper onto him. His hands moved their attention to her fabulous breasts and magnificent nipples. He played with them and sucked on them, smothering them into his face.

Then she started to come, crying into his shoulder. He quickly followed. The motherload, the accumulation of weeks without sex, came pouring out of him with a shriek and a groan that could surely be heard throughout the hotel.

The smell of sweat and smeg and cum filled air. You could almost taste it.

They finished the wine by the neck of the bottle and began again.

This time less urgently.

Slimeball seemed more preoccupied with thoughts of his meeting with Reverened Bob.

Twenty

Reverend Bob had once been a man of the cloth. But it wasn't long before he realised that his calling to booze and women was stronger than his calling to God.

Caught by his parish priest drunk in bed with the church's housekeeper, his calling to Holy Orders was terminated.

By mutual consent.

His short career as an armed robber had been lucrative. Not being a man to push his luck, he took the money and ran, setting himself up in a very nice bar in the town of Fuengirola.

Fuengirola night life is more sedate than most of the coast's resorts. Most people soon find a place which, for some reason special to them, makes it their favourite night-time haunt. Such a place was Bar Reverend Bob's owned and run, of course, by yours truly Reverend Bob.

In his fifties now, with receding hair, Bob was still muscular and handsome. Always smartly dressed in casual summer clothes, he was the typical expat bar owner. A cockney Arthur Daley wide boy character, he had a friendly smile and welcoming way about him.

Word of mouth brought him a steady flow of customers who generally changed fortnightly. He could use the same jokes repeatedly. And he did.

He had been surprised and made curious by the phone call from Colin Simpkins' Serious Crimes Squad, and was looking forward to their meeting. He was intrigued.

Bent coppers were always intriguing.

Twenty-one

Nobody was really looking for David Walker any more. They all thought he was long gone.

The case was still open, of course. The murder by shooting of two Spanish policemen would never be closed.

However, the Spanish authorities were realists. What were the chances of catching him now? He hadn't been seen or heard of in over six months. The last sighting being in Morocco, from where he had fled.

And so, in a quiet corner of a small restaurant in Córdoba with Jane, he felt safe. Holding hands across the table, they renewed their love and acquaintance.

'I know this must be difficult for you, Jane,'

David Walker said, 'but the fact that I have come back for you must prove something to you.'

'It proves you are completely mad,' Jane told him. 'It has to be dangerous for you here.'

David lifted the black bottle of Freixenet 2007 Vintage Especial Brut Cava from the bucket, leaving the ice to rattle and clink in the water, and topped up their flutes.

'No danger, no matter how great, would be worth taking, to be with you again, Jane.'

'Bullshit!' laughed Jane.

'Well whatever...' David Walker laughed too. 'You haven't changed a bit.'

All the old feelings flooded back into Jane's heart and head. The passion they had shared in their brief encounter had been fraught with danger and excitement, like she had never felt in her life.

Against all her instincts and better judgement, she knew that she was going to spend the night with him.

They finished the meal with cheese and a bottle of Sandeman 1966 vintage port. Jane knew that David Walker was back in her life.

Twenty-two

Tiffany Pissed Off was sitting back at her table with a gin and tonic when the kids arrived back. Almost simultaneously her husband arrived from his game of golf and kissed her and the kids. He sat at the table as Pedro took his order for a large beer.

It had been a hard game but he had won.

Tiffany told him how hard it had been for her too, looking after the kids. She exchanged a sly unnoticed smile with Colin Simpkins who was sitting a couple of tables away.

He sipped his beer contentedly, his thoughts intermingling between Tiffany, not so Pissed Off, and Revered Bob.

He observed the happy family scene.

How could anybody really ever trust anybody?

With not another thought for the slut, he finished his drink and went back to his room.

He had to open the windows.

He showered, had a nap, then in the evening took a taxi to Fuengirola.

It was loud and smoky in Bar Reverend Bob's.

Simpkins recognised the Reverend immediately.

Across the busy room they acknowledged each other.

A handshake sealed it.

A drink at the bar, and soon they were talking.

'So what's it about?' the Reverend asked.

'Oh! Nothing much. Just £10 million in gold.'

'I see.'

Twenty-three

Two or three beers along, and we were leaning back in our chairs, reminiscing, dreaming and fortune-telling.

It was a couple of hours past midday when, from our vantage point at the restaurant, we noticed the black stretch limo glide into the coach-cum-car park.

It looked strangely out of place. Even more so when two men, both dressed in black suits, climbed from the front seats and stood almost to attention by the back doors.

As if acting to a huge anticipating crowd, with a flurry of self-importance, out stepped Caviar. I recognised her instantly.

Everybody in the world knew Caviar. Caviar was a global star. An American rock star who had triumphantly conquered the whole world. Arguably, she was the biggest female rock star ever.

A phenomenon. The female Michael Jackson.

But what was she doing here? The last item I'd read about her in the papers said she was doing a massive world tour to promote her record-breaking new album 'A Taste of Caviar'.

Fascinated, I watched as the scene unfolded. Caviar was climbing the hill to the restaurant flanked on either side by her minders. Having made it up the hill and into the open air restaurant, she pushed her $1000 sunglasses to the top of her head and said, 'Hi.'

'A fine entrance you be after making,' grinned Dooly. 'I never seen the likes of it before.'

Caviar laughed. She had a warm friendly smile. Afro-American, she had soft chocolate skin and lush shiny long black hair that fell onto her shoulders just above her sculptured breasts, which undulated down to her moulded hips followed closely by long slim thighs perched upon the most perfect calves in the world.

Caviar was the perfect dish.

She gave me a gaze that melted me like an

icicle in the sun.

'Pretty spectacular eh?' she laughed. 'Who's in the chair?'

'I guess that's me,' I said. 'What would you like?'

'Beer would be great.'

'Beer for me too please, our kid,' the first minder answered in a broad Liverpool accent.

'Me too please,' the second minder said, also with a Liverpudlian accent. 'Hot here, innit?'

Dooly raised a hand to the barman, spread his fingers and called out, '*Por favor señor*, five beers!'

'*Sí.*'

There were only a few youngsters scattered around the bar. It was still early in the day and most were on the water having fun. Nobody really paid much heed to the global sensation.

'Pull up a chair,' I said.

She did just as one of the minders jumped to get it. Five bottles of San Miguel arrived with five glasses.

'Relax, you guys,' Caviar told the minders. 'Take some time out. Cool down and chill.'

Thanking her, they sat at a table a few feet away.

'So what brings a superstar like you to these parts?' I asked.

'Same as you, I suppose,' she answered, casually drinking from the bottle.

'My name's Caviar, by the way,' she said, introducing herself.

'I'm Jack,' I told her, 'and this is my good friend Liam, Liam Dooly. So how's the tour going?'

'It's going really great,' said Caviar. 'Every show is sold out. I've got a few days off between gigs. So I decided to get a look at the real Spain.'

Dooly was building another smoke. 'Well, you've found a right little diamond here, gal. It's my first time here too and I'm lovin' it. But Jack here knows it well.'

'How so then Jack?' asked Caviar genuinely interested. 'What do you do?'

'I'm retired now,' I told her. 'I was in the army for years, then took up salvage diving. I made a lot of money and have a farmhouse south of Marbella. It's a long story, but my thirty-five-foot Winnebago Motorhome lies on the bottom of this lake. I was thinking of revisiting it.'

'You're kidding me!' she gasped. 'Really?'

'No. Honestly.'

'And you, Liam. What do you do?'

'Retired also.' Dooly grinned, lighting up his fag.

'So what did you do then?' she asked.

'I'll let Jack tell yez,' he laughed. 'He's far more eloquent than I am.'

'IRA gunman and hit man for hire,' I laughed.

'*Retired,*' corrected Dooly.

'Now I know you're kidding me,' said Caviar, wide-eyed. 'Aren't you?'

'I fought for the cause in Ireland,' said Dooly. 'A long fight. Most of me young life. Now with the peace process I'm at a loose end. So I'm spending some time with Jack. He still has some healing to do.'

'Healing?' asked Caviar.

'I got badly shot up a few months ago,' I told her.

'Another long story, I suppose,' she laughed.

'Yep,' I said grinning, 'sure is. You don't want to know.'

'Oh, but I do.' She winked at me. 'Let's have a party. I'll order champagne.'

'You'll have to make do with Spanish,' I told her.

'Whatever. Just bring it on, baby!'

Twenty-four

'10 million quid,' said Reverend Bob. 'Fuck me!'

'It's all connected in some way to Jack Reec,' Colin Simpkins told him. 'I don't know how. Nobody does. The man's a mystery. Rolling in dough with no visible sign of support.'

'Like the rest of us, then,' chuckled Reverend Bob.

'Well, you know,' said Simpkins.

'This Dooly character,' the Reverend went on, 'he doesn't sound like one to fuck with.'

'You better believe it,' Simpkins continued. 'A right hard nut. A ruthless killer. A gun for hire. Known to have assassinated Danny "Wonder Boy" McReynolds at Villa Park. Got away scot-free. Clean as a whistle. No trace of evidence.'

'So give me one reason why I should get involved in this?' asked the Reverend.

'10 million quid,' said Simpkins.

'No good to a dead man.'

'I just want information,' explained Simpkins. 'You don't have to be directly involved. You know the underworld around here. Get your ear to the ground and find out all you can about Reec. I know he has that gold. Everything points to it.' He paused.

'There's a big cake on the plate, Bob. And I want my share of it.'

Twenty-five

Caviar had not enjoyed herself so much in years. It was the first time for ages that she could remember feeling so normal.

Normal. Yes, *normal.* Herself.

'Jack,' she said, a little drunk. 'How wonderful a day this has been. Will you be my friend? Please say yes... and you too, Liam. Please. I have so few friends.'

Dooly answered first. 'For sure,' he said, ''tis a fine lass that you are. And coming from Irish blood too.'

'You know about that?' she said with surprise.

'Of course,' said Dooly. 'Your grandfather was a Kerryman. The whole world knows.'

'Caviar,' I said. 'you're a great kid. This is the best time I've had for months. I've been through some bad shit the last year. Do you fancy being normal for a few days. How long you got off?'

'A week.'

'So take a break - a real break.'

'What do you mean?'

'Stay at the farm with me and Dooly.'

'That's crazy!'

'Why so?' asked Dooly. 'You said you wanted to be normal. Or is it all just bullshit?'

'You'll love it. I promise you,' I told her. 'If it's peace and quiet and normality you're after, then there's nowhere like it.'

'So what do you say then?' asked Dooly. 'Let's get it on.'

Twenty-six

The minders were not happy.

One bit.

It took a phonecall from Caviar to the tour organiser to end it.

'I'm the fucking star. It's my life. I know what I'm doing. No, I'm not telling you where I'm going; that would defeat the object.'

'Now listen to me,' screamed the voice at the other end of the phone, 'you can't just —'

'Oh, fuck off!'

'Well, he didn't seem too happy,' I laughed.

'My manager. A cunt. Thinks he owns me. He can get fucked. This is my time.'

'Well said!' howled Dooly. 'One for the road.'

'You guys can go,' Caviar told the minders. 'It's OK. Just split and have a few days off on full pay. The treat's on me. Take no fucking notice of anything anyone says. It's OK. Anyone fires you, just stick around. I'll fix it.'

They shrugged and left. Another bottle of cava landed on the table, and we all howled with laughter as we raised our glasses and saluted the black limo as it glided away from the car park.

Freedom, thought Caviar. But what am I doing? Who are these men? Maybe I'm being kidnapped. What the hell...

Twenty-seven

Pissed, I booted the Jag back along the coast road to the farm. With the roof down the wind tore through our hair, tangling it badly. Caviar sat in the back howling with delight as Dooly mesmerised her with his Irish charm and tales of the old country.

Smiling, I watched in the mirror as they swigged the cava from the bottle. A motorcycle police patrol man smiled and waved while shaking his head in despair as I flashed past him.

He was a colleague of my dearly loved friend Sebastian Aparicio, murdered by that bastard David Walker in Morocco.

I saluted with three honks on the Jag's horn.

It was dusk as we slowed to a stop on the

gravel by the pool at the farm.

'It's fabulous, Jack. I love it!' Caviar exclaimed.

'It gets better,' I said, 'as the night goes on. I'll get things organised. Liam can show you to a room. You can shower and change.'

'I have no clothes, Jack.'

'There are plenty around that will fit you,' I said. 'Liam will show you.'

'I'll take care of it, Jack auld son,' Dooly said as he guided Caviar a little unsteadily to the house.

'See you later, Jack,' Caviar called.

I smiled happily for the first time in a long time. The farm suddenly felt like home again. The emptiness I'd felt since Barbara was murdered was beginning to ease.

It would never go away, I knew that.

But I was beginning to mend.

A start.

When Caviar emerged from the house in one of Barbara's favourite dresses, I cried.

She looked gorgeous.

Just like Barbara.

I cried some more.

'What is it, Jack?' she asked.

Soon she was crying too.

''Tis long story,' offered Dooly.

'Not another one.'

'To be sure. There's many.'

I wiped away my tears.

'You look stunning,' I told her. Then, remembering my other murdered friend, Jesús Alcantara, I asked, 'Have you ever been to heaven?'

'Not yet,' Caviar replied.

'Then let me take you there. I make the best Harvey Wallbanger in all of Andalucia.'

Twenty-eight

'You what?' Zimbalist Jnr, Caviar's manager screamed. 'You crazy motherfucking sons of bitches! You left her with two fucking strangers - in the middle of fucking Spain? Don't you know how much she's worth?'

'But sir,' the Scouse minder pleaded. 'she ordered us to.'

'You fucking stupid assholes. What the fuck you being paid for? Get the fuck outa here. You're fired. Got it. Get the fuck out. Assholes!'

'So what do we do now, our kid?' the one minder asked the other.

'Stick around like she said, I suppose,' the second minder said. 'She said it would be OK.'

'Yeah. I hope so.'

Zimbalist Jnr was panicking like a rattlesnake held behind the head. The biggest, most famous rock star in the world was lost. Maybe kidnapped. For the umpteenth time he phoned her and for the umpteenth time she didn't answer.

He smashed the phone to splinters against the wall. And called the police.

'I know she's only been gone a few hours. Yes, she's not a fucking child. Yes, I know. But it's not my fucking fault, those stupid cunts left her. No, it's not a fucking publicity stunt! She's missing... maybe kidnapped for Christ's sake. Call you in the morning! *Call you in the morning*? Fuck you. I'll call the Press. Now!'

Twenty-nine

We had feasted from the barbecue and now sat by the pool in the warm night air, getting to know one another. An owl hooted nearby, scouring the night in search of a meal. The smells of warm earth, leaves and citrus were thick on the light night breeze.

'Reminds me of home, Jack,' said Caviar, leaning back in her chair with her eyes closed, dreaming momentarily of some far-off place.

'Where's home?' I asked

'Florida,' she answered. 'The Sunshine State. A small neighbourhood called Spring Hill. North up the coast from Clearwater. Beautiful, clean and peaceful.'

'Not as wet as where I come from, then.' Dooly grinned.

'I don't know so much,' Caviar said. 'We too get our fair share of rain at times.'

'Well, there's the difference,' Dooly said. 'We don't get our fair share of sun. Just more than our fair share of the wet stuff.'

'You must come and stay. Both of you.' She sounded excited, just like a normal young girl. 'It would be great. We could hang out. Do some stuff. You know. The beach, boats and things. There's this great place Hudson Beach - Sam's Bar. It's great there, right on the water. Off the tourist trail. The snowbirds don't often find it. You'll love it.'

'Sounds great,' I laughed, 'but as soon as you get away from here you'll never think about us again. You'll be back again in your other world. Concerts, studios, managers and hangers-on.'

'Don't say that, Jack,' she said. 'You're making me sad. Don't spoil everything. I feel so happy.'

'I'm sorry, but—'

'Shush, shush ...please.'

I shushed.

'You were right about one thing, though, Jack. You do make the best Harvey Wallbanger in the whole of Andalucia. And...'

'What?' I asked.

'I can now say that I've been to heaven. I'm going to write a song about it, Jack. I'll call it "I've been to Heaven". It will be your song. Every time you hear it on the radio, you can think of me.'

'And what about me?' said Dooly sulkily, lighting up his roll-up. 'Where's my song?'

Thirty

It was close to midnight and the party was in full swing. Ricky Martin was hammering out his tunes at full blast, and Dooly and Caviar were dancing like 'a pair of eejits', as Dooly would say.

Above the sound of the music I heard the unmistakable growl of a Ferrari engine approaching the house far faster than it should have been going. It braked hard and skidded loudly to a halt, scattering gravel.

It was Horny Formore and Delicious Fantastico.

Welcome guests in anybody's fantasies.

Horny Formore climbed out and in her die-happy voice said, 'Can we join the party, Jack?'

Dooly's eyes lit up like a beacon. 'All sinners welcome here, dear girl.'

The aristocratic beauty of Delicious Fantastico left even the gorgeous Caviar open-mouthed.

'My God! She's amazing. Who is she?'

'A friend.'

Delicious Fantastico held up two bottles of cava.

'We come bearing gifts, Señor Jack.'

'No greater gift could there be than yourselves,' bullshitted Dooly. 'But welcome all the same. 'Tis a hooley then we'll be havin'.'

I don't know about Caviar being in heaven, but I had to pinch myself to make sure I wasn't really there too. With Dooly talking head-to-head with Horny Formore, I was left with the job of amusing Caviar and Delicious Fantastico.

Tough life.

'So how long have you been a kidnapper, Jack?' Delicious asked mischievously.

'Say again,' I said quizzically.

'Caviar.'

'Yes?'

'It is the only story in the whole world, Jack. You must have heard it.'

'Heard what?'

'Caviar, here, disappeared off the face of the planet, this afternoon with two strange men. There's a huge panic going on.'

'That fucking asshole!' exclaimed Caviar madly.

'Who,' I asked.

'Zimbalist Jnr, my manager,' she explained. 'Never misses a chance for some cheap publicity. What are they saying?'

Delicious told her briefly. 'They are saying, señorita, that you went from the lakes at Málaga with two strange men and have not been seen since. There has been no contact with you and they fear that you may have been kidnapped.

'What a croc,' said Caviar. 'I suppose I'd better call the asshole, before he has a SWAT team rampaging through the garden.'

'Well, don't tell him where you are,' I told her, 'or the place will be swarming with reporters and news teams.'

'Don't worry Jack. I'm sorry about this. I just never thought.'

'Don't worry about it,' I assured her. 'Just tell him you're ok and you'll be back in a few days.'

'Sure.'

Caviar went into the house to find and use her mobile phone. I turned to Delicious Fantastico and said, 'She's a real nice kid. Just needs some time out. Grown up far too fast.'

'I understand, Jack,' agreed Delicious. 'I also have grown up far too fast. But it is our life and we all choose what we want to do with it.'

'I sometimes wish ...' I began.

She interrupted me with two fingers placed gently to my lips. 'Don't wish your life away, Jack. But don't waste it away either.'

'Good advice. But what brought you here tonight? I didn't send for you.'

'This one's on the house, Jack.'

Thirty-one

It was going to be a special night. David Walker had planned a grand affair.

He had reserved a room at Hotel Las Dunas next door to the Tikitano Beach Restaurant, Estepona. He had secured the best table in the house by tipping the head waiter generously in advance.

No point tipping *after* the event. It bought you nothing.

Jane looked stunning in a white silk evening dress, and after they were seated he ordered the best champagne in the house. 1997 Louis Roederer Cristal, at €300 a bottle.

Also to have opened to breathe a bottle of red 2001 Pingus, at €990.

Such extravagance! But why not?

'This is crazy,' said Jane. 'What am I doing?'

'Jane. I love you,' David Walker told her, stretching his hand across the table to hold hers. 'What is so crazy about that?'

'I don't know. I just can't think. All that shit. All that killing.'

'It's all over,' he assured her, 'this is our renaissance. We can start again. Be together. You know that's what you want.'

'I'm sorry,' she said, bowing her head. 'It's just that I'm so confused.'

'I know,' he reassured her, 'but just give it a chance.'

'I will.'

'Now let's not talk about it. Enjoy. Don't spoil the evening. It's costing a bloody fortune!'

'I know, I'm sorry. Did you see that about Caviar, the rock star? They think she was kidnapped.'

'I did, yes,' he told her. 'I think it's all a publicity stunt. She'll turn up in a few days and they'll add a few more dates to the tour!'

'That's very cynical of you, David,' Jane

scolded. 'She could be dead for all you know. Then how would you feel?'

'Gutted,' he told her.

They finished their fabulous meal with two glasses of 1966 Sandeman vintage port.

Back at their suite at Hotel Las Dunas, David Walker changed into his comfort clothes and switched on the television. Not unexpectedly, the only story was rock star Caviar.

He watched with interest. He had been in hospital a long time to cure his psychopathic murdering tendencies, and he was cool.

Happy with himself.

He was normal now.

Wasn't he?

But was the fucker in his head?

Only he knew that.

Looking at the face of Caviar on TV, the old urges in his head began to surface again.

He tried to subdue them, but they wouldn't go away.

And then he remembered.

He'd been neglecting his medication lately.

Thirty-two

'This one's on the house, Jack,' Delicious Fantastico had said.

I've never had a better freebee.

As I lay beside her in my bed, her arms wrapped around me, I felt both melancholy and contented. I thought about the past and thought about the future, and thought about Caviar asleep alone in another room.

How could it be that the biggest female rock star in the world was asleep in my home?

She wasn't.

'Come on, you guys,' I heard her call. 'Grub up!'

Delicious Fantastico stirred beside me.

'Jack, my darling,' she moaned, her fabulous naked breasts heaving with the effort. 'Does "Grub up" mean food?'

'It sure does,' I told her.

'Then why are we waiting?'

I could think of a few reasons but I let it pass.

Out by the pool, Caviar was working the barbecue with skill. Bacon and something masquerading as sausages hissed and sizzled as eggs spluttered in deep oil in a frying pan. The smell of freshly made coffee hung thickly in the air.

Dooly and Horny Formore were ably assisting as myself and Delicious emerged into the midmorning sun.

'A hell of a hooley auld son,' Dooly howled. 'You can sure throw a party, Jack. I'll have to give yer that. But the breakfast is down to Caviar here.'

She puffed her chest proudly.

'Just because I'm biggest star in the world and fantastically beautiful, with the most amazing talent, doesn't mean that I can't cook.'

We all laughed.

We knew she was joking.

'Not so much of the fantastically beautiful,' scolded Delicious. 'That's my line.'

I squinted my eyes against the bright sun and my slightly aching head. 'Any cava left?'

'Jack,' said Caviar. 'I've only known you a short time and I'm not as dumb as I look. I opened a fresh bottle and poured it into a jug of iced orange juice. Did I do good?'

'Fucking great.'

The party continued.

Thirty-three

'That is the most amazing story, Jack,' said Caviar, oozing with excitement. 'A plane full of gold at the bottom of a lake.'

'I too find it very exciting, Jack,' Delicious said, contributing to the conversation. We were a little drunk. I was talking too much.

It was mid-afternoon. Dooly and Horny, or was it Horny and horny. were away in their own little world.

A private world.

They looked good together.

Myself, Delicious and Caviar made a great threesome. We talked away excitedly for hours. Caviar had honed her skills as a barista and had fixed us three fresh Harvey Wallbangers.

We sipped through the fresh glistening ice and orange slice, and that's when I said it.

What had been on my mind. 'Fancy a skinny-dip?'

Always ready to please, Delicious whipped off her bottoms and was laughingly pulling down my shorts as I stood up. Caviar looked a little hesitant. She wasn't even topless.

'Come on,' I encouraged her, 'let's have some fun!'

Downing a good half of her Harvey Wallbanger, she leapt to her feet and stripped off her bikini.

Fuck me, did she look good naked! A fabulous chocolate body with a neatly trimmed jet black, ace of spades.

'Jack,' she laughed. 'Is that somewhere to hang my towel?'

We climbed in the pool and cavorted around playfully. Not to miss out on the fun, Dooly and Horny Formore were soon in the action.

As the Reverend Bob watched from the trees, he felt an urgent call of nature coming on. With great gusto he relieved it.

Thirty-four

We all took an early evening siesta. Horny and Delicious showed no sign of wanting to leave.

They were on vacation, they announced. No problem. Caviar had told Zimbalist Jnr she would be back in a few days and to 'butt out' as she put it. She was OK and having a good time.

He didn't like it.

Tough shit.

Dooly was in love.

For fuck's sake!

A besotted gunman!

Whoever heard of that?

Oh well!

I didn't know whether I was coming or going.

Delicious was fantastic, but my giant ego kept telling me what a fantastic trip it would be to make it with the most iconic rock star of the decade...

In a threesome!

Jesus.

Pull yourself together.

'I've done scuba, Jack,' Caviar told me. 'I'm Padi certificated.'

'Well, that's good,' I told her, 'but as a fully qualified instructor I could take you down anyway.'

'So will you, Jack? Please,' she begged. 'It would be the most exciting thing I ever did in my life.'

'OK,' I said. 'First thing in the morning. I've got all the gear. Liam?'

'Yes.'

'Will you be my dive master?'

'To be sure, auld son.'

'Then it's done.'

Desmond McGrath

Thirty-five

It was a mouth-wateringly beautiful morning. It was semi-dark when we started off and the dawn broke across the clear blue sky and the opalescent sea. An orange fiery ball lifted from the waves slowly into the sky, growing larger and brighter by the minute as it burst as a whole blazing ball from the ocean.

Amazing.

Priceless.

It was not lost on Caviar.

'Jack, I just can't tell you.'

We took the Range Rover. Dooly drove, with me as front passenger and Caviar in the back. It was anything but a quiet journey.

Caviar never shut the fuck up. She was like an excited schoolgirl on a day trip. 'Jack, I can't believe I'm going to do this.'

'Believe it,' I told her.

The two-hour drive passed quickly, and soon, just after 5.30 a.m., we cruised quietly and slowly into the deserted car park by the lake.

I felt the knot tighten in my stomach.

Many memories.

Too many.

'OK,' I said jumping out. 'We've not much time. Get kitted.'

Dooly leaned back in his seat and started building up a smoke.

Caviar and I changed quickly into wetsuits and diving gear. Caviar, with some experience behind her, was no slouch. Tanks on, we were soon ready to go.

Dooly lit up.

We entered the shallows and made our last-minute checks and adjustments. Satisfied, we gave each other the thumb and forefinger OK sign and dipped under.

The water was cold and shocked us as it filled our wetsuits. Venting our life jackets, we began sinking as we swam down to deeper water.

We touched bottom at sixty feet. Looming ahead of us was my Winnebago motorhome, now showing the wear of beingunder water for a few years. I could see the excitement in Caviar's eyes through the glass of her face mask.

I let her explore it quickly but we didn't really have the time. The interior was slowly being taken over by algae and plants, which then supported fish. Many fish. In fact it was full of fish.

It was time to move on.

I signalled Caviar to follow me. We swam out of the front door which hung from one hinge, and finned out across the bottom. Following my compass bearing we came to the drop-off. I checked that Caviar was alright. She knew that the bottom would be 100ft. She was OK with that, so we edged over and drifted down.

We touched bottom with a small cloud of sediment. Taking another compass bearing, we struck out across the bottom, leaving a trail of silt behind us that quickly settled.

I could feel and hear my heart beating in my chest. The excitement. The adrenalin. It was always the same. Because every dive is different.

And then we saw it.

Just a shadow at first looming from the darkness but getting slowly bigger and more like a plane the closer we got.

A sunken Lear Jet.

And then we were touching it.

Sam Kennedy was still strapped in his seat, just as he had been when I first found him. His skeletal remains were held together by his clothes, which I noticed were slowly losing the battle. I doubted it was the same fish in residence in his eye socket, but a new inhabitant.

Miguel Lopez, the pilot, was still at the controls, though also sinking gradually to a pile of bones. We let him be and finned slowly to the other side of the plane, where the broken cargo hold door revealed the still spilled fifty or sixty bars of gold.

Jesus. It was still an awesome sight. God knows what Caviar was thinking.

But at this depth we didn't have a lot of time. At 120 feet, twenty minutes was maximum bottom time. And we would be using air fast.

Especially Caviar.

I picked up a bar of gold and gave it to her. I collected one for myself. With the extra heavy weight to haul, we had to increase our buoyancy through our life jackets.

I signed her to get gone.

She followed me. Back to the wall of the drop-off, and up and over. Soon we were finning fast to the shore. We emerged from the water with steam streaming from us.

Dooly was waiting, a fresh roll-up in his mouth.

Eyeing two gold bars, he said, 'Jesus, Mary and Joseph, 'tis a fine sight that youse are!'

After he helped us out, we quickly dried off and changed into T-shirts and shorts.

'We better get out of here,' I said. 'Like now.'

'To be sure, auld son,' Dooly answered. 'to be sure.'

From where he was watching through binoculars The Reverend Bob couldn't be sure.

But it looked to him like bars of gold they were handing over to the Irishman.

Thirty-six

Never before in the whole of her life had Horny Formore experienced such confusion and conflict of emotions.

Dooly also.

Since breaking away from her childhood into adulthood, she had never felt a single thing for a man.

Any man.

Men were bastards.

Especially her uncle.

The one who had abused her.

Raped her.

Repeatedly.

Until she cut his throat.

They never found him.

The hungry pigs at her father's smallholding saw to that.

They devoured every last bit of him as they fought over him in their own shit, until he was shit too.

She always knew she was beautiful and desirable too. What was it to her that men would pay for her body? She'd had it taken for nothing, after all, so why not get paid for it?

And she wasn't selling cheap. The Ferrari proved that. And the fabulous apartment.

She was high class, but time was catching up, and here she was with Liam 'The Slaughterman' Dooly. ex-IRA enforcer and gun for hire.

In love.

Crazy.

Just crazy!

'So have yer ever thought of hanging up yer condoms?' Dooly asked.

'Many times,' she laughed. 'But the money's good and it's a job. I need to secure my future. I'm getting to my sell-by date, and I don't intend going to the bargain basement. You know, reduced to ...'

Dooly laughed at that. 'I don't ever see you in the bargain pages.'

'Well, let me tell you something, Liam,' she said, leaning in to kiss him, 'for you I am a virgin!. The first one I ever gave for free, that wasn't taken.'

Dooly chuckled slightly, some emotion creeping in, a tear spontaneously falling from his eye.

'That's the first tear I ever shed for a woman.'

'Then let it be the last, Liam,' Horny Formore said, taking his face in both hands.

She licked up the tear with her tongue and swallowed it.

'No more tears.'

Desmond McGrath

Thirty-seven

Bar Reverend Bob's was busy that night.

The Reverend was doing the rounds, making everyone laugh, accepting drinks or putting 'one in the till or on the tab'.

Suckers.

But it was Colin Simpkins who caught his eye as he entered the room. With a huge laugh from one of his old jokes, he left his holiday audience and met him at the bar.

'So what have you got?' asked Slimeball Simpkins.

'Dunno for sure,' answered the Reverend Bob. 'I followed them to the Málaga Lakes early, after an all-night party, and to be honest I was totally fucked.'

'And?'

'Well, I watched them go diving through binoculars and I'm sure they came back with a couple of bars of gold. And get this.'

'Yes?'

'I could swear to it that the bird at the party and the one he took diving was that missing rock star, Caviar.'

'What have you been on?' asked Simpkins. 'Gold bars and fucking Caviar!'

'I'm tellin' you, Col, I swear,' the Reverend pleaded. 'I don't really believe it myself, but I swear the cunt was with that Caviar, and that they handed over two bars of gold to that Dooly before they got out of the water.'

Slimeball Colin Simpkins sighed deeply.

As hard as he tried, he just couldn't figure all this out.

Thirty-eight

'How's my song coming along?' I asked.

'Let me take you to Heaven.' Caviar intoned. 'Pretty good. But I could do with a guitar. I need to pick out some chords.'

'Do you want me to get you one?' I asked.

'Sure would be good if you could,' she told me. 'Kinda lost without one.'

'Leave it with me.'

I made a call, and late afternoon, as we sat by the pool with a bottle of cava, I heard the familiar sound of a motorcycle chugging into the yard.

It was Paco Limarez, best friend of Sebastian Aparicio, my dead policemen friend. Paco was also a police motorcycle patrolman.

'*Buenas tardes, señor,*' he greeted me. 'Your guitar,' he said, proudly taking it from his back and holding it up.

'Not *my* guitar,' I corrected him. 'Caviar's guitar.'

'Indeed, a great honour, señorita,' Paco said with all his Spanish charm. 'May I stay a while to hear you play it?'

'Absolutely,' Caviar laughed. 'We're having a party. Can you join us?'

'For sure,' Paco laughed back. 'I am now officially off duty, and Señor Jack throws such good parties.'

'Don't I know it!' Caviar howled, taking the guitar. 'Let's get it on.'

With nothing more than that, the biggest rock phenomenon in the world started playing all her hits, and the whole of the latest album 'A Taste of Caviar'.

Liam Dooly, Horny Formore, Delicious Fantastico and myself, along with Paco Limarez, listened in awe to a multimillion-dollar performance.

And it wasn't spoiled by a duet with Dooly of

'Dirty Old Town' by the Pogues.

And as I leaned across the table to hold the hand of Delicious Fantastico, I just couldn't help but feel that there was a massive spark erupting to a flame-between the dark, handsome young policeman Paco Limarez and the even darker Caviar.

By the end of the night they were becoming inseparable.

Thirty-nine

Caviar was cooking breakfast again.

She loved it.

Paco Limarez was helping.

'Señorita, you have so many talents,' he told her.

'You ain't seen nothing yet, baby,' she laughed, tossing over the bacon and sausages on the barbecue, 'and you ain't so bad yourself! Now, Buck's Fizz. Get me some Buck's Fizz. I think I'm going to cancel the tour and stay with all of you. I've never had so much fun.'

'I also, señorita,' confessed Paco. 'This is surely the finest time of my life.'

'Paco, how long have you been a policeman?'

Caviar asked.

'Since I was eighteen,' he answered. 'Nine years.'

'Do you enjoy it?'

'Sí. I love it. It is all I ever wanted to do.'

'Do you have a girlfriend?'

'Sí. I have many,' Paco laughed. 'In Spain we are very romantic.'

'The women too?'

'Oh no, señorita. Just the men. It is not permitted.'

'How unfair.'

'Not really, señorita. That's just the way it is,' Paco said. 'The woman, she must be spotless and clean, like the wedding dress. You understand?'

'No. Not really. And the man?'

'The man. Well...' He was thoughtful. 'The man... the man, he must be finished with his explorations, then he can settle down and be married and so remain true to his woman.'

'Explorations...' mused Caviar with a wry smile. 'I've never heard it put that way before.

And your explorations, Paco, how are they going?'

'I am still searching, señorita,' he said truthfully. 'I have no map. I have to draw one as I travel. Life is a jungle.'

'Tell me about it.'

I interrupted them at that.

'*Buenos días!*'

'Hi Jack,' said Caviar cheerfully. 'How you doin?'

'Good,' I replied. 'How are you two getting along?' As if I needed to ask.

'I'm picking up a few things about Spanish culture,' Caviar replied. 'Seems a bit one sided to me.'

'Yeah well, that's how it is.'

'Never work in the States.'

'Nothing works in the States,' I said.

'Yeah. So let's forget it,' said Caviar, trying to draw a line under it. 'There are only a few days to go until the big concert, and I'll have to get back for rehearsals and soundchecks. But please hear me out. I love you guys. And I mean, love you guys. You are possibly the only friends I have - true friends, that is. Please, please, please will you come to the concert with me? I really want you to be there. I've never had so much fun. Will you be there? She paused.

'Please don't make me beg!'

Forty

Slimeball Colin Simpkins was still trying to figure it all out.

The Reverend Bob, to be truthful, didn't give a fuck. He was already getting bored with it all.

After all, he had a bar to run. He didn't really need the hassle. And the more he thought about it, he didn't really need Liam Dooly.

But he couldn't stop thinking about one thing.

The gold.

But the stupid thing was that he didn't need it. So why was he bothering. What was it?

Greed.

Sheer greed.

That's all he could put it down to.

Fool's gold.

Sat at an out of the way table in Bar Reverend Bob's, Simpkins and the Reverend talked it all through over beer and cigars. Every now and then Bob would have to raise his glass to one of his fans and accept another couple of free drinks.

The pain of it all.

He had it made, really, he thought. Busy little bar, great flat above. Free food and drinks, as much crumpet as he wanted.

Free!

For fuck's sake, he thought, what was he doing with all this shit?'

Slightly drunk now, Colin Slimeball Simpkins was summing up like a judge at the Old Bailey.

'What we actually know for sure,' he slurred slightly, 'is that Sam Kennedy took his share of the gold on a private jet and disappeared off the face of the earth for nearly thirty years. One of his bars of gold briefly appeared at a jeweller's in Málaga. The jeweller in Málaga passed the information to Mak the Knife. Then he disappeared off the face of the earth too. My guess is that that plane crashed in the lake and Jack Reec found it. And he's the only living soul that knows exactly where it is.'

'Yeah,' mused the Reverend Bob. ''Cause everybody else just seems to disappear off the face of the earth. That's what bothers me.'

Desmond McGrath

Forty-one

Of course we couldn't let her down. Not wanting anyone to know the location of my farm, we met the black limo in Torremolinos.

The two Liverpool security guys were glad to see us. Caviar had seen to it that they kept their jobs as promised.

Myself, Delicious, Dooly and Horny Formore made ourselves comfortable with Caviar and Paco Limarez. Knowing my love for cava, Caviar had done some research, and chilled in an ice bucket was a bottle of Marqués de Monistrol, vintage 2006. Using exclusively the traditional method since 1882, Marqués de Monistrol have developed an exquisite cava. The use of indigenous grape varieties and the extended aging gives this vintage cava elegance, style and finesse.

I popped open the bottle, careful not to waste a drop. Six full flutes, and the bottle was empty. I sipped at it, savouring its magical delicacy. We all toasted Caviar.

'Jack, auld son,' said Dooly. 'You're starting to turn my head with this stuff.'

Delicious Fantastico and Horny Formore were no strangers to the champagne lifestyle. Paco Limarez was thinking he could get used to it too. And Caviar had never been so happy in her life.

'Don't worry, Jack,' she laughed. 'There are loads more where that came from. Crack open another.'

So I did.

Forty-two

Barcelona has so many sights and attractions, from the art and architecture to the parks and gardens, it's no wonder tourists flock each year to the Mediterranean city for a short break or a summer holiday. However, recent years have also seen a new trend in travellers visiting the city-those looking for some exciting concerts! Live music in Barcelona is fantastic. It's a cosmopolitan city that many huge international artists choose as a must-have on their international tours. It was here in Barcelona that U2's recent '360 World Tour' and George Michael's '25 Live' tour both broke the ice.

Palau Sant Jordi is an excellent concert venue up on Montjic Mountain, and a legacy of the 1992 Olympic Games. The multi-purpose site has been filled with water for the World Swimming Championships, covered in ice for

Disney productions, and open aired for Spanish *X Factor* auditions, but is best served as a concert venue. With a capacity of 20,000 for non-sporting events, it's hardly surprising groups such as Green Day, Madonna, Sting, REM, Phil Collins, Beyonce and other superstars choose this venue for the top bill in Barcelona.

It was here at Palau Sant Jordi that Caviar was going to perform and wow the world.

She had arranged suites for us at the best hotel.

'Tax-deductable,' she said, brushing it aside. 'Don't even think about it.'

We had three suites on the same floor, together. Dooly and Horny Formore had one, Delicious Fantastico and me had the second.

And get this! Caviar and Paco Limarez had the third.

What was going on?

Well, Paco looked happy enough about it.

Why wouldn't he?

It was Zimbalist Jnr who wasn't too happy about it. 'What's going down, babe?' he asked.

'Spanish Police,' she told him. 'My personal bodyguard.'

'Yeah. Sure.'

Caviar rolled her eyes. 'Can't be too careful.'

With just over twenty-four hours to the concert we didn't see very much of Caviar. She was rehearsing, doing sound takes and working out the arrangements with her band. She was generally making sure that the show was going to be great.

In the hotel we took full advantage of our suites, not bothering with bars or restaurants, but preferring the convenience of room service.

It was just the four of us. Paco Limaréz the 'personal bodyguard', was never far from Caviar.

The black limo collected us from the hotel and in grand style took us to the concert.

The whole world was watching. Television coverage was global. The paparazzi fought for pictures. The flashes were blinding. Horny Formore and Delicious Fantastico unfolded from the limo and waved to the crowd. Dooly was smoking a build-up with his left hand in his pocket and I was feeling decidedly uncomfortable and slightly embarrassed by it all.

I tried unsuccessfully to shield my face.

But when Caviar stepped out the whole thing went crazy.

Watching the news on Spanish television with Jane, and sharing the remains of last night's 1966 Sandeman vintage port and a cheese board, David Walker was truly fascinated by it all.

Forty-three

Caviar was the global star they had all come to see.

20,000 of them.

And my God, they were not disappointed.

Not one of them.

'And this is a new song!' she roared. 'I've only just written it. We haven't had much time to rehearse it, so you'll have to excuse us if it sounds a little raw. It wasn't intended to be included in the show, but the title track to the next album. It was written by me for a very special friend. And I know what you're thinking. But you're wrong. I mean a *very* special friend. This one's for you, Jack. It's called "Take me to Heaven". And he has. But not in the way all you people are thinking! For Jack!'

The band burst into the intro and Caviar lashed into the song.

My song.

It was great.

I mean fucking great.

Considering they'd never heard it before, the crowd went crazy and jammed to the music. The drummer finished the song with a spectacular solo and 20,000 fans were on their feet screaming for more.

Caviar milked it.

'As somebody once said, it's only rock and roll but I like it, like it - yes I do. Who was it said that?'

The crowd erupted.

'Don't you think that would make a great song too?' she screamed into the mic and then started singing. *'I know it's only rock and roll but I like, like it, yes I do. You know I like it, I like it, yes I do.* Oh my God. What have I done, guys? That's probably going to cost me a fortune in royalties. Have a heart, Mick. Give me a break, eh.'

'More, more, more,' they chanted. 'Again, again, again!'

And so Caviar sang my song again and the crowd just ate it all up.

Me too.

Tears of emotion ran down my face.

Caviar wrote that song for me.

Even David Walker was moved.

He decided to phone Jack and tell him.

Forty-four

Caviar was soaking wet

'How was I, Jack?'

'Sensational.'

'You mean it?'

'Of course.'

'Thanks, Jack.'

'It's true.'

'It means so much.'

'Why?'

'Because it does.'

She threw her arms around me and hugged

me.

Sweatily.

I loved it.

She was great.

The tour was moving to Great Britain: Glasgow, Manchester, Birmingham and three nights at Wembley. As we spoke the whole thing was being broken down and packed into a fleet of articulated trucks. Road crews were feverishly doing their job.

Getting ready for the next leg of the tour.

'The next two months will be mad,' Caviar told me. 'Then it's over. Can I come and see you at the farm?'

'Of course.'

'Can I live there and build a studio?'

'No.'

'Why?'

'Because it's a farm. Not a studio.'

'OK. But I can still come?'

'I said so, didn't I?'

We had a couple of free days together.

Quality time.

We hung out mostly in the hotel bar.

Liam Dooly and Horny Formore were forever engrossed in conversation. Me and Delicious Fantastico were mates.

That's all.

The sex was great.

But nothing in it.

Paco Limarez, however, was constantly at the side of Caviar. They made a great couple. Whether or not he was furthering his explorations or finishing them, I wasn't sure.

But Caviar took every available opportunity to hold his hand. When the time came we all said farewell and went on our way.

The Fab Four, as we now called ourselves - me, Liam, Horny and Delicious - were going back to the farm.

Caviar had a tour to finish.

With her new bodyguard.

And I had a plane full of gold to salvage.

And David Walker had murder on the mind.

A terrible murder.

A murder that would hurt Jack Reec.

The only reason he had let him live.

To hurt him some more.

To kill Caviar.

Part Two

Desmond McGrath

Forty-five

David Walker was cured.

Wasn't he?

He'd been a psychopathic serial killer in the past.

But now he was cured.

Wasn't he?

Well, he supposed he was.

I mean, he couldn't bring the victims back to life.

Could he?

It wasn't his fault they were dead. He was a paranoid schizophrenic, for fuck's sake.

He was two people.

It was the other one who was the killer.

Not him.

He held Jane's hand tenderly across the table.

'I'm so happy, Jane,' he told her sincerely. 'The happiest I've ever been in my life. I'm so glad we found each other again. I thought I had lost you.'

Jane was still confused. David was the only man she had truly loved. Yet she had seen him kill!

Two Spanish policemen.

Right in front of her.

Yes, she believed his excuses.

But she'd seen it.

And then there were Jack's friends, Jesús Alcantara and Sebastian Aparicio.

But he had spared Jack.

Because he wasn't a killer really; they were killed in self defence. When Jack was no longer a threat he let him live.

So he must be OK.

Mustn't he?

It was all too confusing for Jane. She decided to forget it.

'What about Jack and that Caviar, then?' she said. 'How did he ever get involved with her? She's mega.'

'Search me,' said David Walker, 'but that's Jack for you. You know what he's like.'

'And those two women!' Jane exclaimed. 'They are amazing. And Dooly too. He's so cool. Like ice.'

'Yes,' reflected David Walker. 'One to watch, that one. I think I might phone Jack for old times' sake and have a chat...'

But why? thought Jane, and the alarm bells started ringing in her head.

Desmond McGrath

Forty-six

I was back in my comfort zone. The farm. The Fab Four. Tranquillity.

It was a fantastically beautiful clear day. Warm and sunny, with the smells of citrus and heated earth scenting the whole garden. The girls splashed happily in the pool, taking care not to wet their hair, and myself and Dooly luxuriated in it all, with beers and a roll-up and a cigar respectively.

'Tis a great place you have here, Jack,' Dooly told me again. He was always telling me.

'Do I look any browner?' I asked him, laughing.

'You couldn't get any browner, Jack,' he whooped. 'We'll drink to it then: your tan!'

We were slightly drunk.

As usual.

'I'm growing fond of Horny, Jack,' Dooly told me, stating the obvious. 'But it's her line of work.'

'How does she feel about yours?' I asked him.

'I see what you're saying.'

'And?'

'I'd like us both to retire and live happy ever after.'

'Have you told her?'

'Not yet.'

'Are you going to?'

'To be sure.'

'Then get on with it.'

'I will.'

'Good luck, old friend,' I told him genuinely. 'I hope it works out for you.'

'Thanks.'

'You're welcome.'

'And you, Jack?'

'What?'

'Delicious Fantastico.'

'We're just friends, mate. Nothing in it.'

'For sure. Yeah.'

Forty-seven

What a party. The Fab Four. Just us. Loadsa booze! And the food! Well!

Steaks and lamb chops with the fat, sizzling and spitting on charcoal, salad bowls, cheese and fruit and cold meat, and two exotic beauties.

What more was there?

I took a call.

It was Caviar.

She was in England.

Fed up.

She missed us.

Her friends.

We missed her too.

And I had to tell her.

And she cried.

Me too.

'I love you guys,' she told me.

'Hang on in there,' I told her back. 'You'll soon be home.'

'Home,' she said. 'What do you mean?'

'I don't know,' I said honestly. 'I just said it. I mean this is your home. If you want it to be.'

'I do, Jack,' she wept, 'so much. You don't know.'

'Shut the fuck up,' I replied and wept myself. 'You're spoiling my night.'

'Sorry, Jack.'

'Forget it.'

'OK.'

'Just come home.'

'I will.'

'Soon.'

Forty-eight

I was snapped out of my thoughts as two sodden bikinis splashed at our feet.

The two girls were slightly drunk too.

'*Skinny -dipping time!*' they both hollered together.

I shifted the food to the upper grill on the barbecue and ripped off my shorts. Drunk as a skunk, Dooly was with me. Howling with laughter, we ran at the pool and hurled ourselves onto the girls.

Shame about the hair!

Never mind, eh?

The sex was sensational.

Sheer animal lust.

Filthy.

No one cared.

And why should they?

When it was finished and we were all exhausted I suggested we finish the food. In high spirits, we descended on it like hungry hyenas.

Then we rested a while to recuperate and talk.

It was probably an hour later that it dawned on us that we were still all naked. So relaxed with each other we were that we hadn't even noticed.

'It's getting a little chilly,' I said truthfully, looking at my watch. 'It's past midnight. I think we could do with a few clothes on.'

They all agreed.

And then my phone rang.

'Jack,' The familiar voice spoke from the phone. 'What a great concert. How wonderful to see you so fit and well again. We must try and meet up, Jack. Catch up on old times. There's so much to say. I'm really looking forward to it.

See you soon.'

My spine turned to an icicle at the voice of David Walker.

Desmond McGrath

Forty-nine

The voice of David Walker had unnerved me

Even scared me a little.

'Take no heed, Jack,' Dooly assured me. 'He's just a madman.'

'Yes, I know,' I said. 'That's what scares me.'

'He's playing with you, Jack,' Dooly told me.

'Yes. Just like he played with me when he shot me up. Just enough to almost cripple me but not enough to kill me. I don't like being played with.'

'Sure enough, auld son, but what can you do?'

'Fuck all. That's the problem.'

'To be sure, auld son.'

Horny Formore and Delicious Fantastico were going home.

Liam Dooly seemed melancholy. I wasn't bothered. There was no room in my life at the moment for romance.

Just sex.

Nothing in it.

All the same, I was quite fond of my ice cream girl.

'So why don't you retire?' Dooly asked.

Horny answered, 'And how do I live?'

'I can always do the odd hit if needs be.' Dooly grinned, taking a drag of his build-up.

'Not on my account you won't,' Horny told him sternly.

Delicious Fantastico kissed me with more passion than business. 'The Milky Bars are on me Jack.'

They folded themselves into the gleaming red Ferrari, top down, and with a growl of the engine and a hoot of the horn, they scattered gravel up the drive.

And were gone.

For now.

'So where are we at, Jack?' Dooly asked.

'The gold!' I said almost triumphantly. 'The gold. I want to get the lot and stack it neatly like a table by the pool and have the biggest fucking party in the world.'

Dooly chuckled on his fag. 'I've always said it, Jack. You sure know how to throw a party.'

Fifty

It took nearly a month to get it all. Fifty-eight bars. Of solid gold.

I took the last one from the now disintegrating, once proud Lear Jet, and said goodbye and thank you to Sam Kennedy and inhabitants.

I lingered and wondered what things might have been like for him if fate hadn't taken a hand and changed his destiny.

Sun, sea and señoritas, probably, I thought.

Miguel Lopez, the pilot: lost to his family and friends. Gone without trace.

No closure for them.

Yet I had it in my power to end it for them.

But how could I?

I felt sadness and guilt as I finned away from them for the final time with the last bar of gold.

Their gold.

I broke the surface in the shallows, and once again Dooly was there, fag in hand, to take the ingot.

'That's it then, auld son. We're done.'

I pulled off my mask and dragged back my hood onto my neck in a cloud of steam. My face was red and my eyes exaggerated as I climbed out of the water with Dooly's helping hand.

'Sure is.'

I shouldered myself free from my tanks and dropped my weight belt to the ground. Wriggling free of the wetsuit, I towelled off and slipped into shorts and T-shirt.

It was only seven in the morning but the Costa sun was warming. We threw all the gear haphazardly in the back of the Range Rover.

'I am fucking starving,' I told Dooly.

'Me too, auld son,' Dooly confessed. 'How's about breakfast at that roadside bar just the other side of Torremolinos?'

'You bet.'

Gazing through his binoculars, the Reverend Bob said, 'Well, I make that close on sixty bars.'

'Same as that,' said Colin Simpkins. 'Can't be much more. Let's go - I'm starving.'

Desmond McGrath

Fifty-one

The bar-restaurant Rancho Grande was just opening.

It was nine o'clock and it was getting hot. We cruised into the empty car park as a waiter was wiping the tables and adjusting the chairs.

'Hola! Buenos días!' he greeted us.

'Buenos días,' we both said back.

In good English the waiter said, 'It is a beautiful morning, señor, you are out early.'

'We are, auld son,' agreed Dooly, 'and it's starving we are.'

'Would you like our breakfast specials, señor?' the waiter asked.

'Two,' I said.

'And a bottle of yer best cava,' added Dooly, 'with a jug of fresh orange juice.'

'You English...' the waiter said smiling.

'Irish, auld son.'

'What is the difference, señor?' the waiter asked.

'A big difference - to me, anyway.'

The waiter shrugged, 'I don't know. señor.'

And without him saying it, I could read his mind.

'And I don't care.'

But the food was great.

The Buck's Fizz too.

We were just pouring the last of the cava when the hire car drove into the empty car park and stopped behind my Range Rover.

Why do people always park next to you when they have a whole empty car park? It really pisses me off.

Reverend Bob and Colin Simpkins cheerfully walked over and took a table.

Next to us!

Why?

The whole place was fucking abandoned.

'Good morning,' Colin Simpkins greeted us. 'Lovely day.'

'Celebrating something?' asked the Reverend Bob, eyeing the empty cava bottle.

'What's it to you?' sneered Dooly, instantly irritated by the pair of cunts.

'Just making conversation,' the Reverend Bob replied.

'Well, I'm not,' Dooly growled. 'Making conversation, that is.'

'Well, excuse me,' said Reverend Bob, moving to another table. 'We were only being friendly.'

'Thank you and fuck off,' said Dooly.

Slightly alarmed and a little embarrassed, I said, 'What's the matter with you?'

'I don't like that cunt. There's something about him.'

'Calm down!'

'No. I've seen his like before. I can smell it.'

'What?'

'Trouble... big trouble.'

Fifty-two

Dooly hardly spoke all the way back to the farm. When he finally did, he said, 'I don't like that little gobshite. But I don't know what it is.'

'I gathered that.'

'I didn't say anything before, Jack,' he went on, 'but all the time you were diving I always had the uneasy feeling we were being watched. It's a sense you get from the streets. Belfast. Something you can't explain. An instinct.' He grimaced.

'And when those two turned up at the restaurant from the same direction as us, it set the alarm bells ringing. They're scuts, Jack. Believe me.'

I paused to think it over.

'I've great faith in your instinct, Liam,' I told him. 'We'll be vigilant.'

'And the other one,' Dooly snarled. 'He had the smell of RUC about him. A copper.'

'Fuck me, Liam! Calm down, it's only a commercial.'

'Don't mock me, Jack!' said Dooly with menace. 'I've not killed over a hundred men and lived to tell the tale without developing a survival instinct. Those two are fucking shite. And trust me, Jack, if I see them again it will be for the last time.'

I believed him.

He was scaring me.

It came as a relief when my cell phone rang.

'Caviar!' I exclaimed. 'How are you? It seems like forever.'

'For me too Jack. But it's finished. The tour's over. I need space. Sanctuary... The farm Jack.'

'You got it.'

'I know, I'm on a plane to Málaga tomorrow.'

'Alone?'

'Of course.'

'Then I'll be there.'

'Thanks Jack. I've missed you.'

'Me too. And Liam.'

'See ya.'

Fifty-three

She didn't look like an international superstar when she walked through the gate at Málaga Airport.

With plain clothes, dark glasses and a wig, nobody on the Monarch flight from Birmingham recognised her or paid her any attention.

But I knew her.

And after a great hug and a big kiss I whisked her to the open-top Jag where Dooly was in the driving seat.

I sat in the back as Dooly booted it to the farm. Excitedly, Caviar told me everything about the past weeks since I'd seen her. The whole tour had been an amazing success and her albums were selling worldwide. Zimbalist Jnr was not happy at all that she was taking off.

But did she give a fuck?

No!

She'd done her job.

Now it was time out.

Quality time.

Her time.

'Where's Paco?' I asked.

'We couldn't travel together,' she told me. 'As a couple we may have been more readily recognisable. He's having a few days sightseeing in England and following me over at the weekend. I miss him Jack.'

'How is it with you two? I asked.

'I love him, Jack,' she confessed. 'He is just so lovely. Laid-back, you know, unfazed by it all. Cool. I'm just me, to him. Not Caviar. Not a star. Just me.'

'And can I say something?' I asked.

'Sure.'

'He's genuine. Not an act.'

'I know that Jack. You wouldn't believe the shit I've had to take over him. Gold-digger. Parasite. Hanger-on. Everything. I'm pissed with it. I hate people.'

'Calm down! Take it easy. Relax. He'll be here in a few days. Then we can "hang out" as you say.'

'Don't take the piss out of me, Jack.'

Desmond McGrath

Fifty-four

'That fucking Irish cunt scares me,' said the Reverend Bob, sinking a large whisky. 'He's a natural-born killer and I don't like it. I'm outa here.'

'Calm down,' said Colin Simpkins. 'You're not telling me that there ain't enough hard men around here to handle two old men.'

'They ain't fucking old, and they ain't a pushover. I don't know about Reec but that fucking Dooly was born to murder. He's bad news, man, I'm telling you. Fucking lethal!'

Bar Reverend Bob was busy that night but The Reverend was in no mood to be sociable. Not a great host that night.

'Now look,' Simpkins soothed. 'I know you're spooked, but get real. Half the London underworld is living round here. We need four hard men. You're no slouch,' he bullshitted. 'You're as hard as they come on a good day. I can handle myself. Four more tough guys and we've got it in the bag. There are only two of them, for fuck's sake.'

'Yeah,' The Reverend Bob didn't sound sold.

Simpkins poured more courage into their tumblers. 'We hit' em hard. Surprise works every time. For fuck's sake, they're pissed when they're not asleep. We know the gold's at the farm. We'll roll up in the middle of the night and just take it. Six men with guns. How can it fail?'

'I don't know,' said Bob glumly.

Fifty-five

They didn't look like dangerous underworld gangsters, it had to be said.

Four pot-bellied, middle-aged, balding men with an obvious drink problem. Colin Simpkins had to admit to himself that he wasn't convinced he had the right team for the job.

He was beginning to share the concerns of the Reverend Bob.

Vic the Dick, as he had been known in his younger days, was increasingly finding it harder to remember why he got the nickname.

Mad Dog Dan. Well... red face, purple nose, cauliflower ears. Really dangerous.

The fittest looking one of the four, Dangerman, so called after his resemblance to

Patrick McGoohan, could hardly stand up.

The fourth of the motley crew, the Sweeney, was an ex-cockney boxer with great potential, but he'd let it all slide by spending most of his young life behind bars for getting nicked for virtually everything he did. It was his resemblance in looks to Denis Waterman that gained him his name, not his savvy.

The great war council was in session in a back room of Bar Reverend Bob's.

'So what we got then?' slurred Dangerman. 'A half-crippled geezer and an ex-IRA thing. Easy-peasy. Six of us. No probs.'

Mad Dog Dan spoke next. 'Well, Sweeney 'ere can get the artillery, eh, Sweeney?'

'Sure can Mad Dog,' he bounced back. 'Just give me the ordnance.'

'The what?' asked Mad Dog.

'The fucking weapons, you twat!'

'Oh yeah. The weapons. Sorted.'

'I'll get the balaclavas,' said Vic the Dick, all excited.

'Yeah. Great.'

A plan was forming.

They would get some guns and balaclavas and hold up the farm and steal the gold.

Easy-peasy.

'And what we going to do with it when we've got it?' The Sweeney asked.

'We'll worry about that when we've got it,' slurred Dangerman. 'We ain't got it yet.'

Positive thinking, thought Colin Simpkins, growing slightly more concerned.

'So when's the strike?' asked Vic the Dick.

'Whenever we're all sober enough!' howled Dangerman.

The Reverend Bob feared the worst.

Fifty-six

Jane was falling in love again with David Walker. But she was a bit uneasy about it.

He seemed more and more preoccupied with the news and Caviar. She hadn't realised that he was that much into rock music.

But was he?

He seemed just as interested in Jack Reec as Caviar. And their relationship.

But he was so attentive. And adoring. Almost to the point of obsession, she thought. And the gifts. He spoiled her rotten.

And she enjoyed it.

Nobody had ever spoiled her before.

She groaned with pleasure as David thrust into her from behind.

She liked it like that.

Doggy.

Animal fashion.

Raw.

Sinking in as deep as he could he made her cry with ecstasy.

Himself also.

He fulfilled them both at exactly the same moment and they fell away from each other, exhausted, but satisfied.

They were meant for each other. They both knew that. Destiny. Written from birth. David and Jane. It had a ring.

'I've got a very busy week coming up, David,' she told him. 'The hotel is fully booked and most of them are my clients. I won't be able to see much of you.'

'No matter,' he said truthfully. 'I have things to do myself.'

He wanted to see Jack. He wanted to know if it was as he suspected - that Caviar was with Jack.

What was she really to Jack?

How much could he hurt Jack? A lot, he hoped.

Fifty-seven

Spock was Caviar's most trusted roadie and a friend. A flamboyant character, he always cut a dash, in his cowboy hat and boots. - his trademark. Tall and handsome, and smoking thin cigars continuously, he had many times been likened to a young Clint Eastwood.

A grin crept across his face as he heard what Caviar had to say.

With gleaming Californian teeth and tan to match, he laughed. 'Sounds great, babe. Have you asked the band? They need to stand down and chill from the tour. This sounds just what they need.'

'There's no pay,' said Caviar, 'this is vacation time.'

'Understood, babe,' said Spock. 'If you fix it

I'll make it work.'

'You're amazing, Spock. I love you.'

'Me too babe. Let's get it on.'

She had to tell me, of course. After all, it was my farm.

But she needn't have worried. I was always up for a party.

And what a party I thought it would be.

The phone calls were endless, and eventually it all began to slot into place.

Caviar added a new date to the tour - by public demand.

My place.

How was it going to work?

Easy.

The four members of the band were going to travel overland in the tour bus, with their girlfriends of the day. Spock was bringing the small van behind, with enough equipment for a small intimate gig. And Paco Limarez was flying in to Málaga to join Caviar.

Delicious Fantastico and Horny Formore were taking more time out. Much to Dooly's relief and a date was fixed for the concert or party, or whatever it was. I didn't even really know what it was. It was all so surreal.

Spock led the way in the small van with the huge tour bus following. They crunched to a stop on the gravel yard of the farm.

Laid-back Spock, plus cowboy boots and hat, emerged from the driver's door of the van and blew a thin wisp of smoke from his long cheroot.

Caviar ran into his arms.

'Spock! You're amazing.'

She kissed him.

'I love you, man.'

'I know, babe. I love me too.'

They hugged.

'Come and meet my friends. They're special.'

'They must be, babe.' He grinned.

'Shut up.'

She dragged him over to me and Dooly.

'This is Jack and Liam. Spock!'

We all shook hands.

Dooly flicked aside the end of his roll-up. 'I'll have a cheroot, if you got one spare,' he said.

'Sure thing, old man. I got something stronger if you want it.'

'The cheroot will do,' Dooly told him. And with a good-natured laugh he said, 'and less of the "old man".'

'Sure thing. Old man.'

We were all going to get on. I could feel it.

'Don't start without us!' a voice called as the tour bus began to disembark.

Four amazingly handsome young men, all blond, white teeth and San Diego tans, dressed in T-shirts and jeans, enthusiastically greeted us with hugs and back slaps.

Micky, Tony, Dave and Jay.

Then came the girls.

I thought I was going to cum. I think Dooly did.

They all looked the same: Long blond hair. Golden tans. Bulging T-shirts. No bras, and long slender legs in sneakers and skimpy shorts.

Over the top or what!

They just oozed American excitement and enthusiasm.

Tina, Alex, Liz and Val. 'Cool, groovy, what a place! Love it.' Hugs and more kisses all round. I think they liked the place.

'What the fuck do you think's going on?' Reverend Bob asked Slimeball Colin Simpkins as he peered through his binoculars at all the goings-on.

'Search me,' said Simpkins. 'But we'll soon piss on his party when we take that gold. Let's get gone. Things to do.'

Desmond McGrath

Fifty-eight

Vic the Dick, Mad Dog Dan, Dangerman (some hopes) and the Sweeney were all being briefed at their council of war in Bar Reverend Bob's.

A ragamuffin outfit if ever there was one.

It was ten in the morning.

And the booze flowed.

'We'll take 'em completely by surprise.'

'Shoot the shit out of them.'

'There ain't going to be no shooting!' Slimeball Simpkins shouted. 'That's all we need. We wait till they're all pissed, then we go in with the van and load it all up.'

'Yeah,' slurred Danger man. 'Give 'em lots.'

'Quiet, quiet, please,' Reverend Bob called for order. 'Let's keep calm. This ain't gonna be a turkey shoot. Dooly and Reec are no pushovers. We need to be in and out with no clue as to who we are. No talking unless absolutely necessary. The less said the better. A surprise strike. Attack and retreat. In, out and away with the gold. No shooting. I want nobody hurt. That way the police won't be involved. As far as the gold goes, it doesn't exist. Once we've got it it's ours. They can't go to the police and report it stolen. They're *fucked.*'

The Fuengirola Four looked thoughtful at words of such great wisdom.

Sweeney stared into the bottom of his glass as if reading tea leaves. 'Yeah. That's good. I like it.'

Vic the Dick said, scratching it, 'Good thinking, Rev.'

'You ain't as dumb as you look,' howled Mad Dog Dan, laughing at his own joke.

'You couldn't be,' put in Dangerman. 'This is going to be a piece of piss. They'll never know what hit 'em.'

Slimeball Colin Simpkins sighed deeply as he pursed his lips in anguish and doubt. Under the table he crossed his fingers superstitiously.

Desmond McGrath

Fifty-nine

I met Paco Limarez at Málaga Airport and we booted it way past the speed limit to the farm.

It had been the most fantastic experience of his life.

No doubt.

Caviar was great.

He loved every minute and never wanted it to end.

And now he was back home.

And with Caviar.

They hugged and kissed passionately, like lovers.

Which of course they were.

They slid away on their own to a quiet place in the garden and caught up.

Spock set up the speakers and the mikes by the pool and shared his never ending supply of cigarillos with Dooly. The old man.

They really kicked it off together, and were seldom apart, smoking, laughing and drinking together.

Spock only drank cocktails.

Dooly called him a ponce.

Spock told him to shut the fuck up.

Dooly didn't.

But the Ponce and the old man were inseparable.

Spock's stories of life on the road and Dooly's stories of life in the IRA were a fascinating mixture.

They never stopped talking.

The band - Micky, Tony, Dave and Jay - were great guys. No side. Just young American kids living a great dream.

And millionaires too. And the girls. What can

I say?

Tina, Alex, Liz and Val, all late teens or barely out of them, living the dream too.

Shagging their rock star heroes and enjoying a champagne lifestyle.

Yesterday's gone. Live for today. Tomorrow may never come.

It felt good, them being around.

I felt young again like them. I was beginning to forget about the deaths and past tragedies. I was feeling alive again.

At last.

Young people. Young ideas. Zest for life.

I leaned back in my pool lounger and drew hard on my White Owl cigar. I drank some pina colada and closed my eyes in contentment.

And then I heard it.

The unmistakeable sound...of a Ferrari engine.

I pinched myself to make sure I wasn't dead.

Desmond McGrath

Sixty

There was no real pattern to the evening. The afternoon kind of blended into darkness. We ate and drank, each one of us cooking whatever we wanted on the barbecue.

The band and the girls drank mostly beer and smoked dope. Caviar drank cava. Dooly and Spock experimented endlessly with exotic cocktails, and I shared my time over Freixenet 2007 Vintage Especial Brut Cava with Horny and Fantastico.

It was about eleven when Caviar decided to sing. Casually and with ease, Micky, Tony, Dave and Jay took up their positions. Jay behind his drums, the other three with their guitars behind their mikes.

At an unseen signal they burst into play.

They were amazing.

And then came Caviar...

Perfectly, at the exact right second, she began her vocals.

Tina, Alex, Liz and Val danced together at the front. Spock played with his sound deck, pushing knobs up and down. Me, Dooly, Horny and Delicious just leaned back and listened in amazement as they finished the set with my song - 'Take me to Heaven'.

I never even heard the van arriving.

It was only when we were surrounded that I realised what was happening.

The six men were all dressed in black with black balaclavas to match, with the necessary eye and mouth holes. They all brandished AK47 assault rifles. Not the best weapons to be staring down the barrels at.

Only one man spoke.

'No need for anyone to get hurt,' he said. 'We can keep this simple. All we want is the gold. It ain't yours anyway, it belongs to us. There's no point in pissing about, just give it to us and we'll be gone.'

It took some time to register. 'What gold?' I

said.

'Please, Jack, this is important,' the spokesman said. 'This is pointless. We've been watching you for weeks and we know you have it. It's not your gold, but you found it and thanks for that. Now, none of you people here are poor, and I'm sure a few bars of gold aren't worth dying for. So come on, let's be reasonable. And just to show there's no hard feelings, you can keep a few bars for getting it. Could I be fairer?'

I could see the logic.

There seemed no point in arguing.

'It's stacked in the barn,' I told them. 'Fifty-eight bars.'

'Fair do's, Jack,' the spokesman said. 'We'll take fifty and leave you eight. How does that sound?'

'Well in the circumstances I suppose it sounds very generous of you,' I said.

'Good. That's a deal then.' He barked an order.

'Two of you load up the gold. Fifty bars. Two of you guard everyone. Just as a little gesture of your appreciation we'll have a little freebee from the hookers.'

He aimed his rifle at Horny Formore and Delicious Fantastico. 'In the house.'

Dooly jumped to his feet.

I grabbed his arm and held him back.

There was hate and vengeance in his eyes.

I knew they had just made a huge mistake.

Sixty-one

They were gone.

With the gold.

'Liam, it does not matter,' Delicious Fantastico said trying to calm him down.

'It matters to me.'

To Dooly, it seemed to matter more to Horny Formore. She hadn't spoken a word.

Had they been raped?

Or just not paid?

Who could say?

Well, Dooly had made his mind up.

He made a call.

'Dooly? Is that you?' Billy Dufacy answered.

'To be sure, auld son,' said Dooly. 'It's yer help I'll be needing.'

'You've got it, Liam,' Dufacy said unquestioningly. 'What do you want?

Dooly told him. 'Can you find Joe Cahill? He owes me.'

'For sure.'

'I want the two of you over here in Spain with me for a free holiday.'

'Free, Liam?'

'Well, you know...'

'I think I do.'

'I know you do.'

'Want me to bring anything, Liam?'

'Take a guess.'

'I guess I can figure it out.'

'Enough for half a dozen men. For a short campaign.'

'Consider it done, auld son.'

Sixty-two

'Stay the fuck out of it, Jack, if you don't want to know!' Dooly ranted. 'Fuck the gold if you like, but nobody rapes a friend of mine and gets away with it. Got it?' he spat.

'I've got it, Liam. I've got it.' I tried to calm him.

But it was useless.

'We've no idea who they are,' I persisted.

'I know who the fuck they are!' he thundered. 'Those fucking gob-shites we saw at the bar after the last dive. Fucking cunts. I knew they were trouble. Fucking shite. And the one cunt a copper if ever I saw one.'

'But Liam,' I reasoned, 'how will you find them?'

'I'll find the fuckers,' he fumed. 'I took the reg of their car. I knew they were trouble.'

It was Paco Limarez who spoke next. 'Amigo. If you have the car registration number I can easily find you the owner of it.'

'I know that, auld son,' said Dooly, 'and I'm bankin on yer.'

'For sure, señor. No problems.'

Dooly gave him the number and Paco made a call. I knew we were starting some big trouble and I didn't want it. But I had no choice. Liam was my best friend and I had to stand by him. Not to mention the fact of the gold.

The band and the girls and Spock had been shaken up and weren't long in leaving.

Caviar was staying.

She had nothing else to do but go home.

And she wanted to stay.

We all made our fond farewells and wished each other luck. The tour bus, and the van with Spock following, left the farm.

It was the six of us again until the next visitors arrived: the IRA.

Sixty-three

J ane had a busy week and knew she was going to be very tired and irritable. She agreed with David Walker that they should have a week's break and meet after it when she felt up to it again.

David Walker was in agreement. A break would be good. He had a few things to do. And he hadn't felt well just lately.

He knew he was a nice guy really. But he also knew that he was a psychopathic, schizophrenic serial killer, and lately the voice in his head was getting stronger and more persistent.

He knew he should be taking his medication but he also knew he needed the thrill. Of the kill.

One Last Kill.

It had been a long time.

Too long, the voice in his head told him.

Far too long.

He decided on a trip.

Granada is seventy-nine miles from Málaga. Even if you make no other excursions from the Costa del Sol, you should not miss it. With its extraordinary past and flourishing present, it offers what for many is an ideal combination of old and new. Today it is busy with life as a market town and commercial city, but enlivened by being an important conference centre, and home of Spain's third largest university. Monuments, concerts, theatre, exhibitions and a lively night life cater to all tastes. Nearby is the ski resort of Solynieve.

The town sprawls across three mountain spurs thrusting into a large and fertile plain, one of the richest farmlands in the country. Granada was occupied by both Romans and Visigoths, but rose to prominence with the Moors. During the eleventh century it broke away from Cordoba's caliphate to create its own kingdom, and under the Nasrid dynasty (1246-1492) the city developed into one of the most powerful and artistic centres of the Middle Ages.

The priority for most visitors is the sprawling, magical Moorish palace of the Alhambra, where fine arabesque traceries, coloured mosaics, cool colonnades and sparkling fountains greet the wanderer at every turn. Delicate Nasrid architecture, stunning workmanship and sensitive restoration combine to make the Alhambra one of the most remarkable medieval Arab palaces in the world today.

It was here in the backstreets around the cathedral, Plaza Bibarrambla and Plaza Nueva, that David Walker began the hunt.

The Restaurante Alacena de las Monjas, Plaza Padre Suarez. is centrally situated and specialises in local cuisine. Once a rendezvous for the poet Garcia Lorca, Manuel de Falla and other notables, it serves imaginative regional dishes and charcoal-cooked meats.

Twenty euros to the head waiter, and David Walker was sitting at the best table in the restaurant with a bottle of 2004 Chablis premier cru chilled in an ice bucket.

He cut a dashing figure in his white linen suit and soft pink polo shirt. After ordering the house special, fillet steak charred, the waiter poured him a glass of wine.

He savoured its delicate aroma and flavours. It was exquisite.

The restaurant was quiet. It was mid-afternoon. Just as he finished his first taste, a most intriguingly beautiful girl in her mid-twenties entered the restaurant. David Walker raised his glass and smiled. She smiled back.

My God how gorgeous she looks thought David Walker.

What an amazingly handsome man, thought the girl.

David Walker rose from his seat. 'Can I ask you to join me?' he said. 'I'm lonely.'

'Me too,' she replied with a wide infectious smile. 'Why not?'

And the beast in David Walker's head approved too.

Sixty-four

Stealing the gold was one thing.

But rape was another.

The Fuengirola Four were concerned. That was not part of the deal.

The continuous bragging about it and the touting of the photos from their phones was asking for it.

The Reverend Bob and Slimeball Colin Simpkins just couldn't keep their mouths shut. The more they drank the more they talked. It was only a matter of time before they told the world about the gold.

Vic the Dick, Mad Dog Dan, Dangerman and the Sweeney were gradually trying to distance themselves. They might all be washed up, has-been, middle-aged, pot-bellied gangsters, but they still remembered one thing: If fishes could keep their mouths shut they'd never get caught.

They had their share and it was time to get gone.

The car was a hire car.

Paco's friends in the force soon tracked it down. It was hired from Record Rent a Car at Malaga Airport by an Englishman, Colin Simpkins. He had stayed at the hotel Principe Sol in Torremolinos, then was last seen in Fuengirola. He was spending a lot of time in a bar called Bar Reverend Bob's.

The owner was a suspected fugitive from England, one of many living on the Costa del Sol.

'Sounds about right,' said Dooly. 'I think we should pay a visit.'

'Whatever you say,' I sighed.

Sixty-five

The reinforcements were on their way.

The charge had faltered, however, at the Irish Harp Bar in Benalmadena Costa.

Billy Dufacy and Joe Cahill had spotted the place late afternoon and called a tea break to the journey.

At four in the afternoon the Guinness was crap.

At six in the evening the Guinness was good.

At eight on the night the Guinness was great.

At ten it was the best Guinness outside of all Ireland.

Fucking great.

Mother's milk.

More Guinness!

The charge was halted.

An army fights on its stomach.

Bring it on.

T-bone steaks.

Fuck Dooly.

He could wait.

Top shelf.

That was the way forward.

Two Irish whiskeys.

Billy Dufacy and Joe Cahill were pissed.

How it all started neither of them knew. But it did.

Big style.

A woman was involved somewhere along the way; they remembered that.

Just.

Then it was the fight.

They remembered that too.

And trashing the bar.

It got hazy after that.

They remembered being smacked across the head with a baton by the Spanish police.

And now as they groaned back to consciousness in a Police cell, they remembered the car.

Illegally parked.

With six AK47 assault rifles, six Browning handguns, loads of ammunition, grenades and even a mortar, hidden in a secret compartment in the floor of the car.

Shit.

Desmond McGrath

Sixty-six

Caviar just loved the farm.

'Jack, I could stay here forever,' she told me. 'I love it.'

'Me too,' I told her back, 'but I think you should have gone with the others. There's going to be trouble. Whoever they are, they've fucked up big style. Dooly takes no prisoners. When he finds them he'll kill them.' He paused

'No mercy. They've shit the bed. He's a one man killing machine when he gets going and I have to back him. That's the way it is.'

'I know, Jack,' Caviar said, 'but I'm your friend too, Jack, and I want to be there and help.'

How she was going to help I didn't quite

know. But that's how she felt, and I loved her for it. For all her wealth and stardom she was still a down-to-earth American girl.

And she and Horny and Delicious were forming a bond.

Like, friends.

They had shared a bad ordeal together and, like mates do, they comforted each other.

Dooly seemed agitated.

He was pacing around like a caged puma.

The reinforcements should have been here by now.

The last he heard, they were approaching Benalmadina Costa, just a couple of hours away.

Where were they?

Paco Limarez and Caviar were lounging poolside, cocktails in hand and holding hands.

Dooly's phone played a tune.

'Dooly,' he grunted.

'Liam, auld son,' Billy Dufacy answered. 'A small hiccup.'

Dooly cut the call.

'*The fucking eejits*!,' he raged. 'They're banged up in jail and the fucking car and all the weapons has been towed.'

I feared the worst for the campaign and the reinforcements.

'Paco,' called Dooly, 'best pal, good buddy, great friend. Never let you down in an emergency. Do anything for you. Help!'

'I don't like the sound of this, señor. What do you want?'

Desmond McGrath

Sixty-seven

I don't normally speak so easily to strangers,' answered the beautiful German.

'Nor I,' David Walker laughed flippantly. 'But in your case I think I can make an exception.'

'You're so kind.'

'Yes, I know. Some wine?'

'For sure.'

'And what twist of fate do you think brought us together?' he asked.

'I know not,' she replied. 'I only know I am a simple girl who trusts in it.'

And so they shared an exotic meal and some exquisite wine and a few wonderful hours together. As they say, just ships passing in the night.

David Walker knew how to finish a meal. The head waiter had sent ahead for it.

It was breathing.

Ready for the cheese.

Shockingly expensive.

But who cares?

One's last meal should be special.

The head waiter poured and stood back proudly.

1966 Sandeman vintage port.

The best vintage of the twentieth century. It had been an amazing summer crop of grapes.

'People have killed for this,' he told her.

'I'm sure it's worth dying for. It's delicious,' she told him.

'I hope it is,' he toasted. 'To a long and happy life.'

'To a long and happy life,' she repeated.

'*I doubt it,*' echoed the voice in David

Walker's head.

Desmond McGrath

Sixty-eight

'Slaughtered like a pig' was how the headlines read.

The papers and news were full of it. He must be back.

They thought he was gone.

'The Costa Ripper', they were calling him now.

He had stolen her heart.

Literally.

Her heart was gone.

Disembowelled, and no heart.

Prayers were offered all over Spain for the

poor murdered German girl.

How could this happen in a holiday area of this beautiful country?

I watched the story unfold on TV and an icy chill crawled up my spine.

It was him!

I knew it.

He was starting again.

How long would it be before he was taunting me again?

Not long, I suspected.

I was right.

The Spanish courier spoke not a word of English. He passed me the box and I signed for it. I opened it, and it was an icebox filled with melting ice. Inside was a plastic bag containing something.

Meat, it looked like.

There was also a small hand cassette recorder in a waterproof container.

I opened it and pressed 'Play'.

As Dooly held what looked like the heart of a

pig, the tape played. 'I don't like heart, Jack, especially German heart. So have a heart, Jack. Myself, I prefer Caviar.'

Desmond McGrath

Sixty-nine

Paco got them out.

And the car.

He owed.

Someone.

They arrived and Dooly went ballistic.

Gave them a right round of fucks.

Eejits.

Where was all this going, I wanted to know.

Freefall.

David Walker was back sending me the heart of a murdered German girl and threatening the life of Caviar.

Someone had stolen my gold and in the process raped my friends Horny Formore and Delicious Fantastico, and Liam Dooly had called for the IRA to help him with his revenge.

Jesus Christ!

'OK, OK, OK,' Dufacy cried, hands in the air. 'So we let off a bit of steam. Who cares? No problem. We're here now. So what is it you want us to do?'

Billy Dufacy was a laid-back man. Thirtyish, he had seen life. And death.

His one wave of hair was down to his forehead. The rest was neatly combed back and short. He always had a look of mischief and a ready smile.

Joe Cahill was a quiet one. Intensive and deep. Handsome and dark, the same age as Dufacy, he was well known as a ladies' man. His philosophy was simple.

Live life, love life.

Better to burn out than rust out.

'Well, if you've got no tablets I'll have a beer,' he announced. 'Me mouth tastes like an Aborigine's arm pit.'

'Never tasted one,' said Dooly.

'Trust me. You don't want to.'

'I'll take your word.'

'So?'

'Well, I ain't waitin' on yer. Help yourself. The fridge behind the bar. Think you can find it?'

'Bet yer life, auld son,' Cahill said on his way.

'I'll have one too,' said Dufacy.

'And me,' said Dooly.

'Me too,' I said.

'Fuck's sake,' complained Cahill. 'I didn't come all this way to be a fucking barman!'

'Shut the fuck up and get the beer,' laughed Dooly. 'Yer fucking eejit.'

I waved Paco and Caviar over.

It was just past midday. Hot and sunny. We all sat around a couple of tables by the pool with our beers. It was time to sort things out.

The two IRA men listened intently.

'So let's sum it up,' Dufacy concluded. 'The gold. How many times has it been stolen now? Somebody stole it in the first place. Then yer man stole it from the dead man in the plane. And then six men stole it again. From yer man here. And now you want us to steal it back. Again.'

'Right,' said Dooly.

'But,' interjected Cahill, 'they also raped two girls. Friends of yours?'

'Yes.'

'So we got to kill 'em for that.'

'Correct.'

'And in the meantime,' Cahill went on, 'an old friend of yer man here sends him the heart of a murdered German girl and insinuates that he intends to kill the lovely Caviar here.'

'That's about it,' I concluded.

'So presumably you want us to kill him too. Correct?'

'So is this the free Spanish holiday you promised us?' Dufacy's features creased into a smile.

Dooly laughed. 'Just like the old days. You'll love it.'

Seventy

We drank away the afternoon, making plans and throwing ideas around.

I told Paco and Caviar exactly what I thought. She should get the hell out and back to safety in San Diego.

'Jack, I feel safe,' she told me. 'Look at you. The five strongest men I have ever met. How could I not feel safe with you guys?'

'Yes, but if you weren't here he couldn't get you.'

'That's true,' she conceded, 'but it doesn't change the fact that I want to be here, and there's no way he can harm me with you guys around.'

'You don't know the man,' I told her. 'Look

what he did to me! And my friends. He's ruthless and resourceful. Dangerous. A psychopathic murderer.'

'Stop it, Jack. You're scaring me.'

'Good.'

'Don't.'

'Paco. Tell her,' I pleaded. There was enough blood on my hands. 'It's safer for her not to be here.'

'I've told her myself, Jack,' Paco sighed. 'The very same thing. But she is a stubborn woman, señor. She will not listen.'

'Well we'll just have to make sure there's someone with her all the time,' I said caving in.

'For sure señor.'

'I'm making her your responsibility,' I told him.

'I know señor. She already is.'

I left it at that.

So we drank some more beer, cooked food on the barbecue. Each one doing his own. The afternoon cooled down to evening and soon it was dark.

We were all merry in our own way.

I'd buried the girl's heart in the citrus grove.

What else could I do?

I couldn't involve the police.

David Walker knew that too.

So it was decided that the first thing to do was pay a visit to Bar Reverend Bob's. What else could we do?

Desmond McGrath

Seventy-one

It was the sound of Caviar and Paco Limarez making love in the morning that woke me. Not the birds.

Christ they're noisy, I thought, slightly envious.

After breakfast by the pool, we visited the specially adapted car from Ireland and unloaded its illegal goods. We checked the AKs and the Brownings and set them all neatly to one side.

The mortar, I thought, was a bit over the top.

However, you never knew when a mortar might come in handy...

Paco was staying with Caviar and the four of us were going to Fuengirola.

No guns.

Just a look.

We took the Range Rover and parked almost outside the bar. It was just opening. We sat in the vehicle just watching for a while, nothing much happening.

Then we saw a familiar face. Then another one. The two men we had seen at the roadside restaurant the day of our last dive.

Dooly nudged me with his elbow. 'There's the gobshites.'

'I see them.'

'Scum for sure.'

Dufacy spoke. 'They'll know you. It's best if me and Joe go in and see what's what.'

'Yeah, but what you going to do?' asked Dooly.

'Don't know yet. Sniff around,' Dufacy answered.

'Sniff around and what?' Dooly asked impatiently. 'Let's just go in and scare them fucking shitless.'

'Calm down, Liam!' I counselled. 'The boys are right. Take things easy. See what they can find out.'

'I'll give it a go, Jack, but I ain't fucking about. I've got a short fuse. We never fucked about in Belfast, and it got results.'

'This isn't Belfast,' I reasoned.

'Dooly might be right,' said Billy Dufacy. 'We might just tip them off. But I tell you what, me and Joe here will go and play it by ear; you never know.'

A few people were drifting into the bar. It was gone midday and people were ordering lunch.

Billy Dufacy and Joe Cahill wandered in.

'Greetings,' said Dufacy loudly to anyone. 'How's the crack?'

'The crack's a good one in here, Paddy,' the Reverend Bob welcomed them.

'Any Guinness?' asked Joe Cahill.

'Only cans, mate,' the Reverend replied.

'Then cans it'll have to be. Two.'

'Coming up.'

The Irishmen sat at the bar and poured their cans of draught Guinness. The Reverend Bob stood by chatting. He could always spot potentially good customers.

'Here for long?' he asked.

'As long as it takes.'

'For what?'

'To find a place.'

'Looking to buy?'

'To rent first, but to buy eventually.'

'Well, if I can help in any way,' volunteered Reverend Bob. 'I know just about everything there is to know around here. Been here for years.'

'That's very kind of you, Bob,' said Joe Cahill. 'It always helps to have some local information. After all, there are so many con men about these days.'

'Tell me about it,' said Reverend Bob. 'They're on every street corner here. What you guys into?'

'Commodities,' Dufacy answered straightaway.

'What sort of commodities?' Bob asked.

'Anything that looks like showing a profit. We were in property for a time, but saw the crash coming and got out. Made a fortune, so we did.'

'Smart move,' said Bob. 'It's bombed over here too. All the clever money got out.'

'I know,' said Cahill. 'And it's still got a long way down to go.'

And almost as if it were a secret, he leaned across and told the Reverend Bob, 'Trust me auld son. It hasn't even started yet.'

'What?'

'Gold, auld son. Take my word for it, gold is going to rocket. And that's where my money's going. I'm going to buy as much as I can get my hands on. You heard it here first, auld son. Two more cans.'

'On me, Paddy.'

The Reverend Bob's brain was racing.

Desmond McGrath

Seventy-two

Dooly was sick of fucking about. snapped out of my thoughts as two sodden bikinis splashed at our feet

He didn't give a shit about the gold. It was the rape of the girls that drove him.

When Caviar, Paco and Jack had an early night, he told them he was having a drink with the boys.

'OK lads,' he told Dufacy and Cahill. 'Let's sort these fuckers out.'

'I'm with you on this, Liam,' said Billy Dufacy. 'We could spend all year just talking. We'll kill the cunts and finish it.'

'The best way,' agreed Joe Cahill. 'Ye got nowhere fast in Belfast going about issuing warnings. Sometimes the only thing to do is sort it.'

'Well, sort it we will,' snarled Dooly. 'This is personal.'

'I can see that, Liam,' said Cahill, 'and I owe you. It's payback time.'

'Thanks.'

'Let's arm up, then,' Billy Dufacy said. 'A Browning apiece with silencers and one AK in reserve. Just in case. We'll take our own car. Nice and quiet, like.'

'Let's go.'

With one last swig from the bottle of Bushmills they snuck quietly away from the farm.

It was 1.00 a.m. and the bar still had customers when they parked the car just down from the bar.

Dooly stayed in the car while Dufacy and Cahill, wearing sweaters to conceal the guns in their trouser belts, casually entered the bar.

Most customers were now finishing their drinks. Slimeball Colin Simpkins was deep in conversation with four middle-aged, overweight men. The Fuengirola Four, as it would turn out.

The Reverend Bob was collecting glasses and tidying up, while bidding goodnight to the departing customers.

'Good evening, lads,' he greeted. 'You're a tad late but welcome to a drink. Two cans, is it?'

'Nothing else,' beamed Billy Dufacy. 'You better make it three. A friend of mine will be joining us when he's parked the car.'

'No problem.'

There were only the five men at the table and the Reverend Bob left in the bar.

'We're having a little lock-in tonight. Just a few friends. You're welcome to join us.'

'Delighted,' said Cahill. 'I'll just see where my friend is.'

Stepping to the door, he waved Dooly in.

As he stepped inside, there was an instant hush.

Everyone recognised him immediately.

'God bless everyone,' he greeted them cheerfully.

It took them a second or two to gather their wits, the gang of six. They recognised him but of course they knew he couldn't recognise them.

It was just a coincidence.

Dufacy said cheerfully, 'This is my friend Liam. I told him what a great little bar you have here so we've come for a drink.'

The Reverend introduced everyone.

'Haven't we met before?' Dooly asked Simpkins. 'I'm sure I know your face. And yours too,' he told the Reverend. 'Never forget a face.'

Colin Simpkins shrugged his shoulders. 'Can't recall.'

'Sure, wasn't it one morning a couple of weeks ago,' Dooly prodded. 'Out on the road. That restaurant. I was breakfasting with a friend of mine, Jack. Remember?'

'I do recall now,' recalled Simpkins. 'Yes, I was with Bob here. What a coincidence.'

'Isn't it just.'

'How about that,' echoed the Reverend Bob.

Dooly put his hand to his chin and screwed his face up in deep thought. 'You know something,' he said. 'I'm sure we met another time.'

'Impossible,' Simpkins said, laughing it off. 'Too much of a coincidence, that one.'

'I don't think so,' Dooly mused. 'Now, you're going to laugh at this. I know you are. It's just so funny...'

'What's that?' asked Simpkins.

'Well... No, it's too funny.'

'What?'

'Oh, go on then. Have you got a birthmark between the cheeks of yer arse?'

'You what?'

'Have you got a birthmark between the cheeks of yer arse? It's a simple enough question.'

There was an air of panic in the room. The Reverend Bob was getting flustered. 'Now look lads, what's this all about?'

Simpkins was starting to sweat.

It was Joe Cahill who intervened, taking a drink from his Guinness. 'Look lads, let's not get too serious here. There's a simple solution to this puzzle.' He pulled the silenced Browning from under his sweater and pointed. 'You. Show us your arse.'

'What?'

'Show us your fucking arse,' he spat, 'and

quick!'

Dufacy pulled his gun to cover the others as Cahill backhanded Simpkins with an enormous crack that sent him spinning from his chair to the floor.

He stuck the silencer in his face and barked, 'On yer knees, and you just better hope you haven't got a birthmark between the cheeks of yer arse. Because if you have I'll be removing it. Get yer pants down.'

Trembling with fear, Slimeball Colin Simpkins undid his trousers and pulled them down to his bent knees.

'Head on the floor. Arse in the air,' Cahill ordered.

'Well, look at that. Would you believe it? Just like she said,' said Cahill.

'Who said?'

'The girl you raped at the farm when you stole my friend's fifty bars of gold.'

'I don't know what you're talking about,' Simpkins sobbed.

Dooly took up the conversation. 'Well, I suppose I could be wrong. After all, I have killed the wrong man before. But everyone makes mistakes. In your case, though, I don't think so.'

It was Dangerman who cracked first. 'Look lads, I went along with the robbery, I admit that, but I had nothing to do with the women. I didn't like it myself, to be truthful. Not my style. Don't believe in that. I knew it was trouble the moment they did it.'

'Yeah,' the other three all joined in together. all singing the same tune. 'We're all thieves, you understand that. That's the game. But the women, no.'

'I know that, auld son,' said Dooly. 'I was there.'

'You can have the gold,' they all fought to say.

'Sure, I don't give a fuck about the gold,' Dooly told them. 'It's not mine. But I'll take it, of course, for my friend. It's his. The reason I'm here is these two gobshites. They tampered with goods that didn't belong to them. *My* goods. And the sentence for that is the same here as it is in Belfast. Now, how many bullets up yer arse do you think it's going to take to get to your brain?'

Desmond McGrath

Seventy-three

After the German girl, David Walker was out of control.

He was without doubt the maddest fucker he knew.

He should take his medication. He knew that. But then that spoiled all the fun.

And was he having fun!

With the next girl his approach was far less subtle. No wining and dining. No small talk. He just grabbed her from the beach and dragged her into the trees.

He knocked her out long enough to strip naked. Then woke her up as he made love to her. Well, perhaps 'making love' was a slight exaggeration. But he preferred to think of it as that.

As his rhythm built to a climax and he came inside her.

He slit her throat.

Blood spatter saturated him. He made the C-section across her navel then cut up from the vagina to open her up.

As she bled out onto the sand he walked into the sea and washed himself clean. He dried off in the warm night air and then dressed.

With one last casual glance at his victim, he walked to the nearest bar and ordered a beer. It was thirsty work.

He smoked a small cigar while engaging the Spanish barman in casual conversation. He'd been away from Jane for almost a week and was missing her. After another sip of his beer he decided to call her.

She was good.

Just finished the last shift of a horrendously busy week.

Yes. She loved him. And could he get there as fast as possible?

You bet.

Cheerfully, he paid the barman and gave a generous tip. With his bag already in the car, he drove at speed to Jane's.

When he got there she was waiting. The wine was on ice and a tray of nibbles. Happy and in love, they fell onto the bed and had the best sex ever.

When they woke in the morning, lances of sunlight streaked onto the bed through the window. They breakfasted on the balcony with the morning news.

There had been another killing.

The Costa Ripper.

A cold chill and an icy cloud spread over Jane.

Desmond McGrath

Seventy-four

'What the fuck did you bring them here for?' I demanded.

The three Irishmen had brought Reverend Bob and Simpkins to the farm.

'Well, I didn't want to kill them in the middle of town, did I?' Dooly told me. 'Anyway this is where you usually do all of your hangings, isn't it?'

'Only one hanging, and there'll be no more,' I said. 'I'm done with hangings.'

'What's all this about hangings?' Slimeball Simpkins demanded nervously.

'Jack here hangs people in his barn who piss him off. That's all,' said Dooly as a matter of fact.

Billy Dufacy looked excited. 'Jesus, Jack, I've never see a hanging. What's it like?'

'Trust me,' I told him. 'it's not a spectator sport. It's not pleasant. Especially for the poor bloke who's being hanged.'

Slimeball lost it. 'Jesus Christ, you're not going to hang me. Please.'

'Don't be makin' a show of yerself,' said Dooly. 'You're going to die. At least do it with some dignity. I tell yer what; if you're a man about it, I'll shoot you as the rope tightens. Can't be fairer than that.'

That's when Slimeball fell to his knees and begged. Begged and sobbed for his life.

'Stop this now!' I ordered. 'There'll be no more killing here. If you want to hang him, take him somewhere else and do it.'

Dooly was building himself a cigarette. 'Jack, auld son, yer not going soft on me, are yer?'

Joe Cahill was swigging a San Miguel from the bottle. 'I keep hearing all this hanging talk, but it's all about him,' He pointed to Simpkins. 'What about the other cunt?'

'Got a great idea,' said Billy Dufacy excitedly. 'Why don't we just tie their feet and leave their hands free, then hang them both on the same rope, either side of a branch and let them try to hang each other. The one who wins goes free. Genius!'

At that point I lost my patience. 'I can't be doing with this,' I told them. 'Get them out of here and do what you want with them. But don't tell me, because I don't want to know.'

The noise and commotion had woken Paco and Caviar. It was early morning and they emerged sleepily from the farmhouse.

'What is happening, *amigo*?' Paco asked.

Truthfully, I said, 'I'm not sure and I don't care. But it's not happening here. I'm sorry, Liam, but I mean this. Take them away and if you kill them don't come back. I'm tired of it all.'

'Kill them!' exclaimed Caviar. 'But—'

I cut her off.

'None of your business.'

Desmond McGrath

Seventy-five

So they decided to just beat them up.

Badly.

Professionally.

Lots of broken ribs.

The most painful thing of all.

I know. I've had them.

'You know,' said Dooly, rubbing his knuckles. 'you might think you're tough. But where I come from they'd keep you as a pet.'

Simpkins groaned from the floor. 'Can we make a bargain?'

'Like you get to keep your teeth? Sure.'

'The gold,' he grimaced. 'Half each.'

Dooly kicked him viciously in the ribs. 'That fucking gold is Jack's. He found it and he salvaged it. It's fuck all to do with you. Now I'm only saying this once. Do you hear? You give us that gold or you will be screaming to me to end the agony. *Got it?'*

Reverend Bob was bleeding from all of his head. He lay next to Simpkins, gasping for breath, in agony.

'For fuck's sake,' he groaned. 'the gold's no fucking use to us crippled or dead. Use your fucking head for once.'

'Good advice,' said Dooly. 'And I'll tell you another thing, auld son. The only reason you're not dead is because Jack Reec is getting soft in his old age. If it wasn't for him I'd have killed you like the dog that you are.'

His boot crashed viciously into his ribs again. 'I'm getting fucking tired of this.' He stuck his gun right against the man's head. 'One last chance. You're the only thing standing between me and a drink.'

Slimeball Colin Simpkins caved in.

Seventy-six

Dooly, Dufacy and Cahill collected the gold and dumped the badly beaten Reverend Bob and Simpkins at the bar.

Dooly grabbed Simpkins by the throat and pulled him in to his face for the full impact of what he was about to say. 'Believe me, auld son, I think I've made a big mistake letting you live. Please don't prove me right.'

Back at the farm, I was waiting with Caviar and Paco Limarez when they returned.

'I've got the gold,' said Dooly.

'Big mistake, Jack,' said Billy Dufacy. 'You should have let us kill them.'

'He's right,' echoed Joe Cahill. 'You won't have seen the last of them, that's for sure.

They'll come back worse than ever.'

'There's been enough killing,' I told them.

'Sorry Jack, but I disagree. There needed to be two more to end it,' said Dooly, fishing the makings of a cigarette from his shirt pocket. 'Should have been two more.'

'Let's forget about it for tonight,' I said. 'Horny and Delicious are calling in. Let's just chill for tonight.'

The thought of Horny Formore brought a broad smile to the face of Liam Dooly. The growl of the Ferrari engine made it wider.

After all the initial kisses and greetings, it was Jo Cahill who sulked. 'Well it's alright for youse lot, but me and Billy is like two spare pricks at a wedding.'

With wide eyes and an even wider grin, Horny Formore gave a knowing look to Delicious Fantastico.

'You think, señorita, we could find them a friend?'

'Perhaps.'

Horny Formore took her cell phone from her bag and spoke into it.

Twenty minutes later a white open top Lamborghini crunched to a stop next to the red Ferrari.

Two equally gorgeous Spanish señoritas unwound, legs first, from the car.

'On the house, boys,' said Horny Formore. 'My gift to you.'

Desmond McGrath

Seventy-seven

Reverend Bob closed the bar for the day.

Due to illness!

True. Really.

The Fuengirola Four and Bob and Simpkins held a meeting behind closed doors.

It was noisy.

And heated.

Slimeball Colin Simpkins was doing all of the screaming and shouting.

Reverend Bob just wanted to quit.

Get out.

The Fuengirola Four, if the truth were

known, never really wanted in.

'The filthy, dirty, louse-bound bastard!' Colin Simpkins raged. 'Nobody does that to me and gets away with it!' he raged.

'I'll get that fucking gold back and they'll pay if it's the last thing I ever do in my life.'

'If you don't see sense,' reasoned Reverend Bob, 'then I think that's likely to be the case. I'm out. Had enough.'

One after another, the Fuengirola Four murmured in agreement.

'You gutless shower of fuck-ups!,' Simpkins screamed. 'If that's how you want it, I'll do it on my own. I'll find some real men. Men with balls.'

'Please do,' said Reverend Bob, 'because I don't want to know anymore. Just fuck off back to London where you came from and leave us alone. We've had enough. I'm getting too old for this crap. I don't need it, so fuck off.'

Vic the Dick, Mad Dog Dan, Dangerman and the Sweeney nodded in agreement. They just wanted their nice, peaceful, carefree life back. Getting pissed quietly every day in the sun, smoking and having a laugh.

They didn't need this bullshit.

The unanimous vote at the end of the meeting was, fuck off.

And he did.

But he was coming back.

Desmond McGrath

Seventy-eight

Jane was totally confused.

It was happening all over again.

It just couldn't be?

Could it?

It just had to be a coincidence...

Didn't it?

Yet she'd run for her life from him once.

So had she been wrong then, or right?

She just didn't know any more.

Should she just get out?

She'd been quite happy when he was away.

And now he was back she was in turmoil again.

Why?

After breakfast they sat in the warm morning sun on the balcony, not talking very much, both of them thinking.

Jane pondering on things.

David Walker planning how he could kill the biggest rock phenomenon of the decade.

Caviar.

And relishing how much pain it would cause Jack Reec.

Immeasurable he reckonded.

He'd spared Jack Reec for this moment.

He could have killed him.

But he let him live.

To make him suffer more.

It was Jack Reec who had fucked his life up, and by fuck he was going to pay for it.

Death would have been too easy for him.

Death ends pain and suffering.

Too good for Jack Reec.

The man that had fucked up his life.

Desmond McGrath

Seventy-nine

Sonia and Luisa were an instant hit.

Billy Dufacy and Joe Cahill never, even in their wildest dreams, imagined being with two such fabulously beautiful Spanish girls.

Using the fifty bars of gold stacked by the pool as a table, they drank and danced around it. I put on a Spanish CD and the four beauties danced flamenco.

They had no castanets.

Caviar grabbed up her guitar and jammed to the music and danced in a fashion, as best she could to flamenco.

She was going to do a flamenco album.

She was allowed one flop, she thought.

Then again it could be great.

Who knows?

It had never been done before.

The food sizzled and spat on the barbecue and the cava and cocktails flowed. Everyone was getting drunk. Dooly built some fags and gave them round to Billy and Joe. I found a cigar somewhere and Dooly struck a match on 5 million quid's worth of gold.

Fuck me, I thought. 5 million quid stacked by the pool. Probably the world's most expensive table.

The Spanish CD fell silent and Caviar did some stuff. Not the usual stuff, but softer, melancholy ballads. We all just listened in awe, and knew what it was that made her the global star that she is.

A star that would shine forever, even into old age.

Little did we know then that David Walker had other plans for her.

And they didn't include old age.

Eighty

There was a storm raging in David Walker's head now.

He could sense Jane's anxiety.

The voices said *kill.*

But he loved Jane.

She was the only woman he had ever loved.

It just wasn't fair.

He couldn't bear to think of her in fear or pain.

Suffering.

So he waited until she was asleep to slash her throat.

It felt good.

Knowing that she hadn't felt or known a thing.

Died in her sleep.

The way we all would wish to go, really.

Free now of Jane's encumbrance, he set to making his plans. While she bled out onto the bed, he was packing his belongings and preparing for the journey to Jack's place.

And then suddenly he felt sad.

He was sorry for what he had done.

But he had to do it.

He covered her with a blanket.

Picking up his bag, he moved to the door.

Looking back at Jane for the last time, he closed the door behind him.

He was on his way to Jack Reec and his destiny.

Eighty-one

Back in London, Slimeball Colin Simpkins wasted no time.

He knew the two brothers he wanted and went straight to them. Two up-and-coming East End gangsters, they were reputed to be the next Krays.

Hard, ruthless, merciless.

Just the ticket.

The Maloney brothers: Dennis and Dave.

Two right fucking spivs.

Short and fat, Dennis thought he was Jack the Lad. A little man with a big chip on his shoulder. The older of the two.

The younger brother, Dave, was even uglier.

As someone once remarked, 'I think his mother must have dropped him out from the top of the ugly tree. And he bounced a few times on the way down.'

And what they lacked in looks they sure didn't make up for with brains.

Thick as pig shit.

'Fifty bars of gold,' Dennis said thoughtfully. 'That must be worth thousands.'

'Must be,' reiterated Dave. 'Thousands.'

'Yeah,' said Simpkins, wondering if he was really doing the right thing.

'So what we gotta do, then?' asked Dennis. 'Just take it back off 'em?'

'And who's got it, then?' asked Dave. 'A farmer and a thick Irish cunt?'

'Yeah,' said Simpkins.

'Easy-peasy, old son!' laughed Dennis. 'Let's get it on.'

'Yeah, let's,' said Simpkins.

Eighty-two

Sonia sucked expertly on Billy Dufacy's-hard on. Just when she felt it coming she stopped.

And watched it twitch and throb. As she watched it ease, she licked again around the rim until she saw it start to throb again.

'You like, señor?' she asked as she brushed her dark brown nipples across his thighs.

'Jesus, Mary and Joseph!' he groaned. 'Is this pleasure or torture?'

'You tell me, señor,' Sonia purred. 'For me it is pleasure for sure. You like me to sit on it?'

'Give me a minute.'

'No problem.'

It was still rock solid, but the throbbing had subsided. She knew the time was right. Licking it one more time, she raised herself up and sat on him. Taking it in her hand she rose up again and placed it inside her.

She wriggled a bit with it in until she was comfortable. Bending forward she kissed him. Then she got a rhythm going. Up, down, left, right.

Then Billy started to thrust.

Harder and harder.

Deeper and deeper.

As much as he enjoyed the sight of Sonja, he couldn't hold his eyes open. Eyes squeezed tight, he moaned.

Moaned in ecstasy.

Cried out in ecstasy.

Screamed in ecstasy.

'Fuck, fuck, fuck!' he cried. 'Holy Mother of God!'

Like a funfair ride slowing down Sonia eased to a stop.

'You like?' she asked.

Billy Dufacy couldn't answer.

'I think so, then,' Sonia answered for him.

It was a similar story all over the house.

Happy days.

Eighty-three

Another kill.

It hit me like a sledgehammer.

Jane.

The tour guide.

David Walker's lover.

I couldn't believe it.

I told the others everything.

'He wants to kill Caviar. He wants to hurt me. You've got to go,' I told her. 'He's a madman. Dangerous. A real crazy.'

'No, Jack, I'm safe here. I know it,' she told me.

It was the quiet one, Joe Cahill, who spoke next, thoughtfully, as he drew on a roll-up. 'She's right, Jack. It'll take some man to get through us five. We've got the guns and stuff; I think we should get them all out and get prepared. If he's going to come we need to be ready.'

'He's right, Jack,' said Dooly. 'She'll be safer here than anywhere. We know she's in danger. Anyone else will think it's just pie in the sky.'

Paco Limarez said, 'I agree, señor. If he is really coming, then this is the place I would choose to be and the people I would want to be with.'

'Well said,' Billy Dufacy joined in. 'From now on there must be always two of us awake and on guard. You know him best, Jack, so tell us all about him.'

I did.

I told them how he murdered Barbara, my girlfriend. Cut her up. I told them how he shot Sebastian Aparicio in the back in Morocco, and killed Jesús Alcantara in the darkness of the abandoned boatyard.

I told them how I thought I had burned him to death in the inferno of the boat shed.

I told them how he had completely

outsmarted me and deliberately spared my life and shot me in both legs and my shoulder.

I told them how he somehow made a clean getaway from Morocco and was never seen again. I told them that above all he deserved respect. In fact he demanded it.

'Take him for granted, drop your guard and you're dead,' I told them.

'David Walker is your worst nightmare.' And they all fell silent.

Desmond McGrath

Eighty-four

Spock came back.

Caviar loved that.

He was her friend.

She'd missed him and it was good to see him.

They hugged and kissed and he told her how he had been worried about her. He'd taken the van back and caught a flight straight back to Málaga. He hired a car at the airport and here he was.

'Was that OK?' he asked.

'Of course,' said everyone.

Flamboyant as ever, he mixed us cocktails.

mai tais.

Good. Real good.

At the same time, Slimeball Colin Simpkins and the Maloney brothers were on their way to Bar Reverend Bob's in Fuengirola.

While not that pleased to see them, Bob quickly agreed to get them what they wanted.

MAC 10s and handguns.

No problem.

Anything for a quiet life.

With his fond memories of Jane safely stored in his mind, David Walker drove towards his date with Jack Reec.

It would be a long drive, and when he got there it would probably be a long wait. He stopped at a *supermercado* and bought some essential supplies. A bag of ice for the cool box, lots of tins of food, bottles of wine and beer, and a bottle of Blue Label Smirnoff vodka and some tonic water. He also purchased a small gas cooker, a frying pan and a small saucepan.

All in all, about, enough stuff for a week's camping. He found the farm easily enough and picked his spot carefully to set up a makeshift camp.

Knowing the wind would mostly be blowing from the mountains, he positioned the camp down from it so that any smoke and cooking smells would travel away from the farm. It was early evening when he had finally made himself comfortable.

Parked in a small clearing in the citrus groves, he lit the gas burner and prepared to fry some fresh chicken legs in his brand new frying pan. With his Swiss Army knife, he pulled the cork from a bottle of local red wine and poured himself a glass. He turned over the chicken in the sizzling fat and looked through his binoculars at the goings-on at the farm.

All seemed normal.

The bar was open, the food was cooking and the music was playing. Everyone having a good time. He leaned back on his elbow and drank some more red wine. He enjoyed surveillance.

Took him back to his days in Special Forces. The watching and the waiting. It gave him time to think. To plan. To prepare.

Gave him a buzz. A big buzz.

The sky was clear and the moon bright, the great clean aromas of the pure Spanish country air felt thick in his nostrils. He breathed deeply and enjoyed it. Turning the chicken in the boiling oil for the last time, he drank more wine.

He was slipping into that comfortable and contented feeling.

Happy.

One Last Kill.

Then he would seek treatment again.

Get cured once and for all.

And next time he would make sure to take his medication.

Eighty-five

The first morning of surveillance, David Walker noted that the red Ferrari and the white Lamborghini left with the four fabulous women, any one of which would make a great murder date for the crazy beast in his head.

That left six men and the vic: Caviar.

Surveillance was boring.

Caviar was sitting with the bloke in the cowboy hat strumming a guitar and writing things down.

Writing a song, probably.

The bloke in the cowboy hat was drinking what looked like an exotic cocktail. The others and Jack Reec were just drinking and laughing.

But they were armed.

Taking no chances, he thought.

And who could blame them.

He'd sent them the girl's heart, after all.

It was going to be a long day.

He had some cold chicken and salad and he was hungry.

He opened a bottle of red wine and settled down for what he knew would be a long vigil.

But he had them in his sights.

Just one mistake. Just one opportunity...

That was all he needed.

Eighty-six

The Maloney brothers were tough. They knew that. Cool customers.

They were looking forward to giving it 'Large' to those thick Irish cunts and the has-been, shot-up old soldier, Jack Reec.

Candy from a baby, was the thought that sprang to mind.

Slimeball Colin Simpkins was reserving his judgement. But the element of surprise was on their side.

They'd never expect him back.

So soon.

They'd planned it all down to the finest detail, then decided to play it by ear.

Surprise and MAC 10s.

No answer.

We'd done a rota for guard duty.

Taking no chances with David Walker, we were prepared. It was me and Liam Dooly to guard the perimeter for the first half of the night. Billy Dufacy and Joe Cahill would be the second shift.

Spock and Paco were left out of contention. No disrespect, but Spock didn't know one end of a gun from the other, and Paco Limarez, even though he was a trained Spanish policeman, had never shot a gun in anger, let alone killed anybody.

So we kept it to the four of us.

David Walker was enjoying the last of his fresh food. a T-bone steak that he could eat with his hands. In between bites he drank some red wine and checked on the farm.

All seemed peaceful. The usual. Drinking, eating, smoking. Two bodies fewer tonight. But probably in the house resting. The juice was running down his chin as he took another mouthful from the fillet side of his T-bone. As he washed it down with red wine he was startled by the sound of rapid automatic gunfire. He threw the bit that was left of his steak over his shoulder into the trees and grabbed up his binoculars.

There were three men holding MAC 10 machine pistols on the four men and the girl - Caviar.

As the men threw their hands in the air, from somewhere there was a resounding explosion of gunfire and the three men with MAC 10s began jumping and bouncing and falling in all directions.

Everyone was scattering.

The girl and cowboy hat and another ran for the house. The other two grabbed up guns and started shooting quite unnecessarily at the men on the ground.

From left and right, still firing, Dooly and myself entered the arena.

With the speed of a cheetah, David Walker seized his opportunity. Running like a greyhound, he was down to the farmhouse in seconds.

He knew where he was going.

Straight to the house.

The gun was silenced.

He saw the three of them as he burst into the kitchen.

The gun coughed and he shot cowboy hat. Straight between the eyes. Paco Limarez turned in shock just in time to see the puff of smoke that blew him to eternity.

David Walker punched Caviar straight beneath the chin and caught her before she hit the ground. Scooping her into his arms and throwing her over his shoulder without pausing, he was running back the way he came.

Hardly raising a sweat or breaking breath, he tossed Caviar into the car and was gone.

Eighty-seven

We stood over the bodies.

'Fuckin eejits!' spat Dooly.

'Where's Caviar?' I said.

'In the house with Paco and Spock,' Joe Cahill told me. 'They beat it quick.'

'Good,' I said. 'I just can't believe they came steaming in here like that. They must be fucking crazy.'

'Fever, auld son,' Dooly told me. 'Gold fever. I'll go find Caviar. What you want to do with these?'

'Bury them for now,' I told him. 'I'll get Paco to arrange for Sebastian's cousin at the crematorium to get rid of them properly.'

'Move them from here, Jack,' Dooly told me. 'We don't want Caviar to see them. I don't think it's her scene.'

'Right,' I said. 'Give us five minutes, then fetch her.'

We dragged them away into the barn. Then Dooly went to the house.

When he came back he was ashen.

'Jack, they're dead.'

'Who?' I panicked.

'Paco and Spock.'

I was in total shock.

'They've been shot. And Caviar is gone.'

Eighty-eight

We couldn't keep this to ourselves.

It was too big.

We called the police.

The whole fucking world descended upon the farm.

The biggest monster in the world had taken the biggest star in the world.

That had to be the answer.

It was the only answer.

Wasn't it?

David Walker!

It had to be.

I was in shit street.

Nothing in my life had ever been as bad as this.

Nothing.

The biggest fuck-up of all time. A shit storm equal to no other.

I just cried.

Dooly tried to console me.

'Jack, it's not your fault.'

'The fuck it is! You know it is, Liam. Leave me alone. Please. There's nothing you can say. This is my worst nightmare. Nothing can come close to it.'

'I know, auld son. I'm sorry.'

Police vans, police cars, helicopters. News crews. Television crews. Reporters. Management. Record companies' media moguls.

Did I want an agent?

How much for my story?

Would I write a book?

At least half a million in advance.

Just fuck off! Leave me alone...

'Serial rights - that's the way forward', I heard. 'Don't sign with anyone before you've spoken to Max Clifford.'

'I'm not signing with anyone!' I screamed in sheer frustration. 'Fuck off and leave me alone.'

'Where do you think she is?'

'Do you think she ran away?'

'Is it a publicity stunt?'

'Could she be kidnapped?'

'Is she dead?'

Unthinkable.

I cried some more.

Desmond McGrath

Eighty-nine

When Caviar came around she was frightened.

But she tried not to show it. She was in the passenger's seat of David Walker's car with her wrists bound.

She wasn't gagged. So she spoke. 'Why are you doing this?' she asked. 'If it's money you want... no problem. You can have it.'

'I don't need your money,' David Walker told her.

'So why then?'

'It's a long, complicated story,' he said. 'I'll tell you later, over supper.'

He was driving through the night with a

purpose. His old campsite in the hills. Fresh water, fresh fish and fresh rabbit on tap.

It was the only safe place.

Where there were people there was danger.

Isolation was safety.

And peace too.

And right now it was peace and tranquillity that he wanted. He smiled at the thought of the nickname he had given himself. *El Conejero* – the Rabbit Man. He had killed and eaten so many while hiding in the hills before.

He found his old campsite easily. He found the large outcrop of rock by the small stream and parked behind it. The moon was full and bright, as he remembered it from before.

'Will you try to escape if I untie your hands?' David Walker asked.

'Where to?'

'Good point.'

He unbound her.

'So what's this all about?' Caviar asked. 'Will you kill me?'

'Probably.'

'Great!'

'But there's no rush.'

'Just gets better.'

The normal David Walker smiled.

He was liking Caviar.

She had spunk in her.

Not his, yet.

But soon.

'I'll light a fire,' he said. 'It gets cold. I'll gather some leaves and wood.'

'I'll take a pee,' Caviar said. 'I'm pretty desperate.'

'I'll leave you to it.'

'Thanks. Appreciate that.'

'You're welcome.'

Over a couple of plates of tinned beans and sausages they spoke like murderer and victim.

'Like some wine?' he asked. 'Not great, but drinkable.'

'Sure. Why not?' said Caviar.

'Mind it from the bottle?' he asked. 'Can't be arsed to find the glasses.'

'OK by me.'

He had a swig and passed her the bottle. 'Good health.'

'Some hopes.'

Ninety

I told the world about David Walker.

Everything.

It was now the biggest story in the universe.

I watched Sky News at the farm with the three Irishmen.

The newsreader was a man called Peter Philips.

'It has to be the most shocking story of the decade. Caviar, the biggest rock star of the century, kidnapped from a farm in Spain.

'Spock Wall, her Roadie, shot dead, along with Paco Limarez, her Spanish friend and constant companion. Mystery also surrounds her 'new friend' Jack Reec a dubious character if ever there was one. With no visible means of support, he leads the lifestyle of a millionaire. How was it he came to be involved with Caviar? Rumour would have it that they met casually at Málaga Lakes in Spain and became friends. Or was it more sinister than that? Did Reec contrive to make a meeting with Caviar? Was he involved with her abduction? We pass you over to Emma Griffiths on the ground in the Costa del Sol. Yes, Emma, what can you tell us?'

After a second or two's break in transmission, Emma's voice came on. 'Yes, Peter. Mystery surrounds Jack Reec. An ex-soldier and veteran of the Falklands War, he seemed to drop off the radar until he appeared here on the Costa del Sol, apparently loaded with money. An ex-salvage diver, rumours abound of recovered treasure trove and drug running.

'However, the police or tax authorities can't shed any light on his apparent wealth. Add into the mix his association with ETA and the IRA, and we have unfolding the makings of a great James Patterson thriller.

'Liam Dooly, William Dufacy and Joseph Cahill are all known killers. Liam Dooly in particular is strongly suspected of the Villa Park assassination of Danny 'Danny Boy' McReynolds, and subsequently the killing of his father, Sean. And still the big question remains. What was Caviar doing with known killers? And the even bigger question is… Where were her minders? How could this have happened?

'And what does Jack Reec and the IRA know about it all? I leave you with all these questions. Emma Griffiths, handing you back to the studio from the Costa del Sol, Spain.'

'Yes, thank you, Emma. Indeed. interesting questions. Who is this Jack Reec, and what are his connections to the IRA. Investigators have also uncovered that a well-known local gangster, Mak the Knife, and his gang disappeared without trace after a rumoured run-in with Reec.

'There are many unanswered questions.

'And the biggest one of all is, are Jack Reec and his gang behind the disappearance of Caviar? And are the Spanish authorities up to the task of finding out?'

Ninety-one

Caviar read somewhere once that the best way to stay alive in a kidnap situation was to try and build a relationship with your captor.

And to be honest, she found it easy with David Walker.

In fact she liked him.

Crazy.

She knew that.

But hey. what was there to lose?

'So what turned you into a murdering monster?' she asked.

David Walker laughed loudly. 'The monster in my head does the killing. Not me.'

'So can't you get rid of him?' Caviar said.

'I tried, actually,' David Walker confessed. 'But there's something about him.'

'You need help, man.'

'Had it.'

'Like to try some more?'

'Maybe.'

'Like, just for me?'

David Walker laughed out loud again. 'You know, I'll think about it.'

'Please do.'

He did think about it.

And how much he liked Caviar.

They finished the bottle of red. from the bottle, and opened a second. This time he fetched the glasses from the car.

Also in the car he found his medication. He liked Caviar so much that he took some.

Piling more wood on the fire, they welcomed its heat and drank the second bottle. Then talking away, they drifted to sleep.

Ninety-two

I turned off the TV.

'There's a shit storm coming,' I said, 'hurricane proportions.'

'We've got to get rid of those bodies.'

Dooly finished rolling his smoke and lit it. 'Jack, auld son, there's no way we can risk shifting them. We'll have to bury them deep, as far out from the house as possible.'

Joe Cahill said, 'They'll be swarming all over the place now. I can't believe they think we had anything to do with it.'

Billy Dufacy's mouth creased into a broad grin. 'You've got to be kidding! They know Dooly killed the McReynolds, but they've got no proof. You and me are known IRA enforcers, and Jack here is as dodgy as they come. Who else are they going to be looking at? This David Walker could just be Jack's cover story, for all they know. Who's ever seen him?'

I sighed deeply. 'He's right. Get rid of those bodies and bury them as deep and far away as you can. If ever they find them we're in shit street.'

Cahill and Dufacy did just that.

Just in the nick of time.

The big guns of the Spanish police descended on the farm.

And the interrogation was ruthless.

But what could we tell them but the truth?

When they left I don't think they were entirely convinced but they had nothing else.

At least they were off our backs for a while.

The next lot along were Caviar's people and the army of investigators they had hired.

No expense spared there.

Ex-FBI, CIA, special forces...

And they didn't seem too particular about how they got their information.

Ninety-three

Todd Chandler was hard.

He pulled Dooly into his face by his shirt and almost spat it. 'You'll tell me everything I need to know, you little Irish shit.'

'Is that so?' Dooly said, crashing his nut onto Chandler's nose. It crunched and gushed blood all over Dooly's face. 'Well, maybe I will, if you talk to me nicely.'

Dooly short punched to the stomach with enormous force that doubled Chandler. To help him straighten up, he kneed him under the chin. Chandler crashed onto his back on the floor.

'Dear me. I think you need a refresher course in interrogation.'

He lit his roll up. 'What do you think, lads?'

Billy Dufacy and Joe Cahill looked thoughtful.

'Think you could be right, auld son.'

'What say we start again?' Dooly said, offering his hand to help Chandler up.

I shook my head slowly. Slightly out of disbelief and slightly out of admiration.

Ninety-four

El Conejero – the Rabbit Man - was at it again. With a snare he had made from some wire and a stick, he had caught a rabbit.

He'd caught it cleanly.

Round the neck.

A quick death.

He hated it when they suffered unnecessarily. He loved animals and hated killing them.

But if it was for food he could justify his conscience. Using the handle of the car jack as before, he spit-roasted it over the open fire.

Caviar sat eagerly awaiting the meal.

She was hungry, and as a country girl herself she had no qualms about eating the rabbit.

David Walker was calm.

He had taken more medication that day.

He loved it in the hills, living the outdoor life. Trout for breakfast, rabbit for supper, fresh spring water and warm sunshine.

What else was there you could possibly want? Just Caviar...

'I suppose you can have sex on plate as an international superstar,' said David Walker casually.

'I can have sex on a plate just being a woman,' Caviar replied.

'Do you like sex?'

'Yes, I love it.'

'Would you have sex with me?' David Walker asked.

'Do I have a choice?'

'Sort of.'

'What does that mean?'

'Well, I would prefer you to enjoy it.'

'And if I don't?'

'That would be a pity.'

'Do you think I might?'

'Most do. Some don't.'

'I like sex best when I'm drunk.'

'Me too. No rush. We can eat and have some wine. I bet you never ate out like this before.'

'Actually I have, at home,' confessed Caviar.

'I'm feeling really horny,' said David Walker. 'You're a really sexy, gorgeous girl.'

'I know,' said Caviar. 'Got some more of that vodka?'

'Sure.'

'Then let's have some.'

They were sexed up.

Half a bottle later they were naked.

'In the stream,' groaned Caviar, tongue in Walker's mouth. 'I just love it in the water.'

Like two wild animals they went at it

rampantly. Caviar found a large rock and hoisted herself onto it. David Walker held tightly onto her waist with both hands as she raised her bottom and spread her legs.

She opened herself up and helped him in. With wild enthusiasm he set to his task.

Unselfishly.

This one was for Caviar.

He wanted her to want more.

And she did.

Easing off as she came, so as not to come himself, he brought her back again.

And again.

And again.

And again.

Until he could stand it no more.

He fired off inside her, screaming at the sky to God knows who, and rammed her until it was all gone.

David Walker was empty.

Caviar full.

They were both exhausted.

In the morning they did it all again.

Desmond McGrath

Ninety-five

S ky News told the story. Worldwide.

'Concern turns to panic,' began Peter Philips, 'as there is still no sign of singing sensation Caviar. The mystery deepens, with no ransom being asked. Has she been murdered? Is it a publicity stunt? And rumours abound that retired FBI agent Todd Chandler went from the house of Jack Reec straight into an ambulance and was taken to the emergency room. Emma what can you tell us?'

'Yes, Peter, I can confirm', Emma Griffiths began, 'that a perfectly healthy Todd Chandler entered the house of Jack Reec and a very unhealthy-looking Todd Chandler was helped from the house into an ambulance. I am here in the midst of a media frenzy outside the farm-house belonging to Reec. The Irishman Liam Dooly emerged briefly, and when questioned by reporters replied, and I quote, "That fucking eejit has got as much jurisdiction here as Old Mother Hubbard. And to coin a phrase, when he got there the cupboard was bare," unquote. So yes, Peter, the mystery thickens. This is either the most elaborate publicity stunt of all time or a tragedy of Shakespearian proportions. Yes, Peter, this is rapidly turning into a murder enquiry. Handing you back to the studio, this is Emma Griffiths from the Costa del Sol.'

'Thank you, Emma. Indeed a mystery. And one that may never be solved, as faith in the resolve of the Spanish authorities fades.

Do they really care? The big question is already being asked. This is Peter Philips, *Sky News*.'

Ninety-six

'Got any ideas?' I asked Dooly in the kitchen of the house. snapped out of my thoughts as two sodden bikinis splashed at our feet

'I got one,' he told me. 'I'm getting rid of that shower of shite camped outside the house.'

'That sounds a good one,' I told him. 'What you got in mind?'

'You won't like it so don't ask.'

Dooly left the room and didn't come back.

Then I heard his voice.

Outside.

'This is private property. Get off it. Now.'

Then I heard the full magazine of a MAC 10 machine pistol empty into the sky.

They left.

As far as the end of the drive.

Joe Cahill and Billy Dufacy were in agreement.

Me too.

'This isn't Belfast, Liam,' Dufacy said.

'You're just creating more problems,' said Cahill.

'I think we need to get the fuck out of this place,' I told them all. 'It's just too crazy for me here.'

'You're the only one that knows him, Jack,' Dooly said. 'So where do you think he is?'

'I think he's gone to ground. Out in the hills. He can live off the land. He's trained for it. He doesn't need shops. He's trained in survival. And well practised.'

'OK then,' said Dooly. 'Let's go out and find the bastard.'

Ninety-seven

We disappeared quietly, the back way. While they were camped out on the road.

Just in time, by the sound of it.

I could hear the howl of the sirens getting louder.

Even in Spain, you can't go firing off a MAC 10 on TV and expect to get away with it.

'So what do you reckon?' Dooly asked.

'Where he went the last time,' I said. 'We couldn't find him then, so it won't be any easier now.

'And where would that be?' asked Dufacy.

'South. Way down south. Within striking

distance of Morocco. Down by the Straits. That's where he'll be. I know it.'

'So that's it then,' Joe Cahill said. 'And by the sounds of it, we better get a shift on.'

We did.

Ninety-eight

'We need Finn McCooll,' Billy Dufacy announced out of thin air.

'Finn McCooll,' I exclaimed. 'Who the fuck's Finn McCooll?'

'If we were talking the old Wild West, I would say he was the best tracking woodsman in the world. Never had a roof over his head. An outdoor man,' Dufacy told me.

'Finn McCooll!' I repeated. 'So how do we get him?'

'Finding him's one thing,' said Dufacy. 'Persuading him's another.'

'Just tell me will you,' I said impatiently.

'He'll be in Galway somewhere.'

'Then phone him,' I said.

'Finn McCooll's got no phone. One of the boys will have to track him down. And wait for his answer.'

'Just do it, then.' I told Dufacy. He made his call.

Ninety-nine

Finn McCooll flew into Faro in Portugal.

It was closer to us than Málaga by far. He crossed over the border on a package deal to the Costa de Luz.

We collected him.

He didn't wear buckskins or a Davy Crockett hat, but I feel sure in a previous life he would have.

He was definitely not a return ticket.

Never all there.

'Hello Paddy!' he greeted us.

There was no Paddy there.

'Is that yerself I'm talking to? To be sure. To be sure it is.'

I wasn't sure.

'So who's the dude we're looking for?' he asked.

I told him all about him: David Walker.

'Ah. Yes,' he said, as if he completely understood. 'I'll need a detailed map of the whole area. A good one.'

'You've got it,' I told him.

And when he had it he pored over it for hours. Demanding no interruptions.

We'd rented a small empty villa weekly and made one massively big shop to last us a month. The less we were seen the better.

'Villa' was probably incorrect. It was really an isolated small cottage, a finca, in Spain.

Not daring to interrupt the thoughts and investigations of Finn McCooll, we sat in the shade of a large umbrella covering our table, with beers, waiting for the great man to say something.

Eventually he spoke. Great words of wisdom.

'Hello Paddy,' he began.

Never right!

'Yes?' I answered.

'There are four approximate areas I would choose if I was him. He needs fresh water, shelter and shade. Fresh fish. Fresh meat. Rabbit! Wood for a fire. Isolation from humans. Somewhere he feels safe yet close enough to civilisation that he can get a few worldly goods, like booze and stuff. Are you with me?' he asked.

I was.

'So these are the places I think he might be,' Finn continued.We all listened eagerly.

Desmond McGrath

One Hundred

Peter Philips began the news broadcast.

'In an incredible twist in the disappearance of rock star Caviar, suspect Liam Dooly was filmed firing an automatic weapon to scare away news crews from the farm belonging to Jack Reec. And when police arrived to investigate the incident, the farmhouse was abandoned.

'There was no sign of Jack Reec, Liam Dooly, William Dufacy or Joseph Cahill. Emma Griffiths is at the scene. Yes, Emma. What can you tell us?'

'Yes, Peter, it's an incredible turn of events. Discharging a MAC-10 machine pistol, Liam Dooly forced the news crews to flee, making it more likely by the minute that Jack Reec and his Irish gang of killers are in some way involved. The theory still is that this could be an elaborate publicity stunt. But if it's not... well! Emma Griffiths handing you back to the *Sky News* studio from the Costa del Sol.'

'Thank you for that, Emma,' Peter Philips resumed. 'We have here live in the studio Caviar's manager Zimbalist Jnr. Zimbalist, what can you tell us? The world wants to know.'

Zimbalist Jnr cleared his throat. 'I can tell you on behalf of Caviar's management team that this is no publicity stunt. Caviar met Jack Reec while on a break between concerts and struck up a liaison that I can categorically say was against my wishes and without my approval. I can't understand what got into her. And that Irish killer! Well, I'm lost for words.'

'So you don't think Reec is a good influence?'

'A good influence?' he exclaimed. 'The man's a gangster!'

'That could be deemed as slanderous, Mr Zimbalist.'

'Then let him sue me.'

'Well, we have to leave it there for now. It seems that Caviar's management did not approve of her choice of friends. If what they say is correct, then things look more and more like an abduction. And in the event of no ransom demand, can we expect to find a body? The body of Caviar?'

One Hundred and One

'So where are we going with this?' Caviar asked. She was scared.

She'd seen her best friend, Spock Wall, and her lover, Paco Limarez, shot dead before her very eyes.

But she didn't want to die too.

She wanted to survive.

To live.

With the guilt, yes.

But to live.

That was the important thing.

To live.

And she had so much to live for.

'Do you want to ransom me? If that's all, no problem, my people will pay... Handsomely.'

'No, that's not it,' said David Walker, turning the rabbit over the fire. I don't need your money. I have enough of my own.'

'What, then?'

'Right now I don't know,' David Walker answered her. 'But take comfort in the fact that I am taking my medication and do not feel the urge to kill you.'

'Great.'

'I think the rabbit is done,' said David Walker. 'More wine?'

'Please.'

Caviar could use a gun. She was American. Everyone in America could use a gun.

David Walker was careless with his.

If only she could get her hands on it.

Then she could kill the bastard.

One Hundred and Two

Todd Chandler emerged from the hospital to a barrage of cameras and microphones, reporters and film crews.

'Where is Caviar?'

'How could this have happened?'

'Where is Jack Reec and his Irish gang?'

'Do you expect to find her alive?'

'Have you any clues?'

'Where were her minders?'

'Is she dead?'

'Has a ransom been demanded?'

'How much?'

'Will they pay it?'

'Is Jack Reec behind it?'

'Is it the Real IRA? They're back in action. They killed two British soldiers. They started to bomb again. Do they need funds? Is it them?'

Todd Chandler lost his cool.

Understandably.

He lashed out at the nearest camera, sending it crashing to the ground.

'How the fuck do I know?' he shouted. 'Get the fuck out of my way!'

Knocking over the nearest reporter, he pushed his way through the baying mob.

'Will you be organising a hunt to find her?'

'What do you intend to do next?'

'Have you got a plan?'

'Of course I've got a fucking plan!' he screamed. 'Just get the fuck out of my face.'

He broke through into the open door of a limousine and drove off at speed.

Emma Griffiths stood aside from the crowd and spoke into her microphone as the crew filmed.

'So there you have it, folks. If my interpretation of events is correct, then I don't think anyone has a clue as to the whereabouts of Caviar. Also Jack Reec and his gang of Irish killers. All I can say is, God help Caviar. Will we ever see her alive again?

'This is Emma Griffiths handing you back to the studio from the Costa del Sol.'

Desmond McGrath

One Hundred and Three

We drove to the hills and made camp in the first area that Finn McCooll had thought a possible place for David Walker to hide.

We gathered firewood and cleared an area by the stream of stones and rocks to make a smooth flat area where we could sit and sleep. We laid out our sleeping bags and started a small fire for warmth and comfort.

Not being true hill men, we got out our Calor gas bottle and cooker. With a saucepan full of beans and a frying pan full of steaks, we opened the red wine.

'Needs to breathe a while, auld son,' said Dooly. 'I think I'll have a Bushmills.'

Dufacy and Cahill murmured in agreement.'

I took a beer.

Finn McCooll threw back a Bushmills, then washed it down with a swig of San Miguel.

'Hello Paddy,' he began. 'Sure it's not NASA, so it's not. In these hills there are four predominant brooks, streams or rivers. Call 'em what yez likes. All we have to do is one by one follow 'em up to the top. And if I'm right, somewhere along the way of one of them we find yer man.'

I had to admit that, as simple as it sounded, it was logical. I waited for him to say some more.

He didn't.

He was finished.

There endeth the lesson.

One Hundred and Four

David Walker was tickling trout on his back by a rock pool and flicked one out over himself onto the ground.

He didn't like to think of them gasping for water like a drowning man gasping for air, so he immediately killed it with a rock to the head. Then he set about catching one for Caviar.

The sex had been great again that morning.

At first he thought she was only doing it to survive, but then he began to realise that she was enjoying it too.

And why not? Caviar was enjoying it. She had to admit. And why not too?

She hadn't got much else going for her at the moment. But she had to admit she was enjoying the outdoor life. She watched David Walker as he gutted the fish and encased them into the campfire to cook.

'You can really be such a nice man, David,' she told him. 'I find it so hard to believe that you can kill so easily.'

'I was trained to do it,' he told her. 'It was my job once.'

'Who did you work for?' Caviar asked.

'The British Army. Special forces.'

'SAS?'

He nodded.

'Wow! Must have been exciting.'

'One way of putting it, I suppose,' he said wistfully.

'Yet you're so kind to animals,' she probed. 'How is that?'

'Apart from cats, most animals only kill to eat. Not for pleasure. They are worth more than most human beings. Human beings kill for pleasure, for money, for sex, for revenge. Murderers are likened to animals. That insults the animal. Hunters kill for sport.' He winced.

'What sport is there in killing a tiger with a

high-powdered rifle from half a mile away? If hunters want sport, let them get a knife and fight the tiger. That's sport.'

'Wo. wo?' said Caviar. 'Far too deep for me.'

'Too deep for most,' said David Walker.

'So why do you kill?' Caviar said. 'What's your excuse?'

'I only kill for survival or when threatened,' he said. 'The person who kills indiscriminately is not me.'

'So who is that person?'

'I wish I could tell you. I don't know. But he has ruined my life. He takes me over sometimes and I am totally in his control.'

'Is there any chance you could get rid of him for a bit, then?' Caviar asked.

'I think he's sleeping at the moment,' said David Walker smiling. 'Well, can you try not to wake him?' Caviar smiled back.

One Hundred and Five

We fried our breakfast in the pan and Finn McCooll mud baked a trout in the rekindled campfire. When he thought it was done he poked it from the fire with a stick and cracked it apart with a stone. It broke open, revealing pink steaming flesh.

It looked delicious.

With a fork he picked the flesh from the bones. Finishing his fish, he said, 'Hello Paddy, how's the crack?'

I made it my business to find out who this Paddy was.

'So we'll let the camp stay and we'll do a little exploring. We'll follow the stream both sides and do some recce work out from it. He may not be camped right by the water but just close

369

enough to it. Are you with me?

We were.

We spent the whole day climbing the stream to its source at the top of the hill and searching far and wide on either side of it for the trace of a campsite.

There was none.

We made our way down and it was evening when we got back to camp.

'Hello Paddy,' said Finn McCooll, his usual start to every announcement. 'It would for sure have been too much to hope for that we'd find him at the first place we looked. More likely than not it is always the last.'

From experience I was inclined to agree.

One Hundred and Six

Todd Chandler was not as dumb as he looked. He couldn't be!

Caviar was potentially worth hundreds of millions of dollars to Zimbalist Jnr and her record company.

Todd Chandler had been given an open chequebook.

And a million dollar bonus if he brought her back safe and well.

Big bucks!

He'd hand-picked three top men, all ex-CIA or FBI, and while he was in hospital they were expertly tracking the movements of Jack Reec and his Irish gang.

When they reported that Reec and his men had made camp at a remote site in the andalusian hills.

With no sign of Caviar.

He was on his way.

If Caviar wasn't with Jack Reec, then he knew for sure that Reec was looking for her.

And he wasn't camped in the middle of nowhere for nothing.

He must have some clues. know something. Todd Chandler hired a car and drove to join the other three where they had made a camp overlooking Jack Reec and the Irishmen. He turned off the radio. It was interfering with his thoughts.

It was increasingly obvious that Jack Reec didn't have Caviar. But what clues did he have? What information did he hold?

How could he get that information?

He suspected that he couldn't. Reec was no pushover. And the Irish-men. He'd found out the hard way about them.

He decided to just track them. He had no clues of his own. So that seemed his only hope. Let them do the hard work and find Caviar, then he would take her from them.

It all sounded so easy. But he knew that it wasn't.

He drove on through the warm evening, climbing away from the populated areas. He followed his instructions and drove deeper into the hills. The light was nearly gone now. Soon it would be dark. It started to feel a little cold. He put on the heater in the car. He knew he must be close now. Using his cell, he spoke to them. They guided him there.

To where they were waiting.

Desmond McGrath

One Hundred and Seven

Peter Philips sat at his desk and began *Sky News.*

'This is the eight o'clock *Sky News* and I'm Peter Philips. Serious fears are now growing for the safety of global rock phenomenon Caviar. There has not been one single word from her in the three days since she disappeared - or if you believe Jack Reec and his IRA gang, kidnapped by some mysterious and further more unheard of serial killer.

'And now Jack Reec has disappeared with his Irish friends. Zimbalist Jnr, Caviar's manager, tells us that he has hired ex-CIA and FBI agents to track them all down. But so far it seems with little success.

'There are scenes around the world of fans screaming and crying in distress. From America to Britain and even as far as China, the outpouring of grief is immense.

'They seem convinced that she is already dead. Candles are being lit all around the globe. Prayers are being offered in churches worldwide. What can you tell us, Emma, over on the Costa del Sol?'

'Yes, Peter, I can tell you that hope is fading fast here in Spain. The authorities here are not used to such crimes. It never happens in Spain. As in the case of Madeleine McCann in Portugal a few years ago, the police seem helpless as to how to proceed. I have been told that they are calling in Scotland Yard for help.

'In fact I am informed that they have a senior officer Colin Simpkins from the Serious Crimes Squad, already on the Costa del Sol, although reportedly he's on sick leave. However, extensive enquiries have failed to locate him. Calls to expats in the region reveal that he was involved in some way with Jack Reec. Colin Simpkins seems to have disappeared off the face of the earth - a common phenomenon it seems where Jack Reec is concerned. So the mystery deepens.'

'This is Emma Griffiths, handing you back to the studios.'

One Hundred and Eight

Todd Chandler ground his car to a halt at the campsite in the hills.

Frank Klugman, his former FBI ex partner, greeted him. Frank had Jewish blood and looked and spoke the familiar Jewish way, even though he had never been to Israel.

The other two, Al Gordino and Sly Moreno, were CIA, ex. Both were of Italian extraction, Gordino more so than Moreno. Gordino was third generation pure. Moreno was a bit of a mixture.

A mongrel.

A dangerous mongrel.

'What's going down, then?' asked Todd Chandler.

Frank Klugman answered. 'Don't rightly know,' he said truthfully. 'When they made a break from the farm we followed them. They've been camped here for a day and spent yesterday travelling upstream, exploring.'

'Tracking?'

'Seems that way.'

'They obviously don't have the girl, but they know who has,' said Todd Chandler. 'Maybe she has been taken by a psycho killer.

'Could be.'

Al Gordino overran the conversation.

'I've been studying the map,' he said. 'I think they're following a hunch. If they figure that whoever has the girl is hiding in the hills, then they're following procedure to find them. Whoever it is needs food and water. There are only three sources of fresh water in the area. They've eliminated one already. I saw them. So maybe instead of following them, we should leapfrog them.

'Forget about sleep tonight and overstep them to one of the other two likely sites - the only other two water sources in the area.'

Sly Moreno gave his spin on things. 'He's good, ain't he?'

One Hundred and Nine

D avid Walker could see them a mile off. 'I think we've got company,' he told Caviar.

He'd been keeping up with the news on the car radio and knew that there was a posse of former FBI and CIA agents searching for him.

He zoomed in on them with his high-power binoculars.

He smiled inwardly to himself, quite amused by them. They looked exactly what they were.

Prats.

The sunglasses!

OK.

But the suits?

Well!

FBI, CIA, the news had said.

Well, he'd shit them.

From the moment he had seen them he knew they didn't have a hope.

Fucked.

He would pick them off one at a time.

In his time.

'I think your rescuers are coming,' he told Caviar.

'Who says I need rescuing?' said Caviar. 'I'm quite happy here as I am. I love the open air life.'

'You're such a professional,' said David Walker. 'I could almost believe you. A true survivor.'

Caviar shrugged. 'To the end.'

'So what do you think I am going to do with you?' he asked.

'You, or the other guy?'

'Good question.'

'So?'

'Me, I like you,' he told her truthfully. 'The other guy, I don't know.' 'Just keep taking the tablets, I say,' Caviar laughed.

David Walker laughed too. 'I will, I promise.'

'Well thank God for that.'

One Hundred and Ten

Having used the night to leapfrog Reec and the Irishmen, Todd Chandler and his team spent the next day exploring the second option.

Nothing.

So if they were all on the right track, it had to be the third stream, the deepest in the hills.

So that was where they went.

And that's where David Walker had seen them.

And now it was he who was the hunter. Not them!

'It's not that I don't trust you,' he assured Caviar, 'but I'm going to have to tie you up.'

'Will it hurt?'

'Only if you fight it,' he told her. 'If you just sit quiet and wait for me to come back there will be no problem.'

'OK,' Caviar said, holding out her arms. 'Tie me.'

He did and sneaked off into the night.

With his knife.

And his gun.

David Walker was now SAS.

Doing what he loved.

What he was trained for.

Combat!

He decided straight away that they were sloppy.

No idea that they were the hunted and not the hunters.

They sat around their campfire smoking and sharing a bottle of Southern Comfort and beer, laughing and joking as he watched.

Silently and patiently he waited. Until one of them needed a leak.

It was Sly Moreno who raised himself from the ground, and as he walked towards David Walker, began unzipping his flies.

While he was still pissing with his cock in his hand, David Walker clamped his mouth and expertly slit his throat and lowered him gently to the ground.

David Walker slipped quietly away.

He could hear them calling.

'Sly! You OK man? That must be one hell of a piss!'

When he didn't answer they were slightly alarmed.

When they found him they were shocked.

And scared stiff.

Desmond McGrath

One Hundred and Eleven

Finn McCooll took the point.

Lead tracker.

'We're following someone, he announced. 'Four sets of feet. Big feet. No girl.'

'How do you know?' I asked.

'It's me fucking job. That's what you're paying me for.'

'Fair enough.'

'Could be anyone, though,' he said.

Dooly gave his spin on things. 'We're surely not the only ones looking for her,' he said.

'I know,' I said, 'but who would think of

387

looking out here?'

Dooly shrugged. 'How do I know? Perhaps we were followed. I don't know. But one thing's for sure, we're not the only ones out here.'

'I think we need to be more alert,' Billy Dufacy said. 'I think we need to do a watch at night. Keep an eye.'

Joe Cahill agreed. 'Can't afford to get sloppy. Seen it too many times at home. Sloppy to dead. Quick as a flash.'

'I get the message,' I told them. 'Three hours each night watch. No booze on duty.'

'OK.'

They all agreed.

'There's something up,' said Finn McCooll from the front. 'There's a campsite ahead.'

He waved them back.

'I'll take a look.'

Quiet as a mouse, he snuck ahead. All caution, barely breathing. He slipped his handgun from his belt and held it ready. He poked the campfire with a small stick. It was just barely warm, and a tiny wisp of smoke drifted from it with a little white ash.

It had been used the night before and that morning. The campers were gone. All but one.

The one who they had tried to conceal or bury under a pile of rocks.

Finn McCooll pushed away the rocks where he guessed the head would be. Sly Moreno's throat was slashed open, clean as a whistle.

He was already starting to decompose. The sun in the hills was relentless. Finn rolled the rocks back over the head and called us over.

'Slit throat.'

It was late afternoon.

'Might as well camp here,' Finn McCooll went on.

'Slit throat,' said Billy Dufacy to noone in particular.

'Who and why?'

'I've got a pretty good idea,' I said. 'David Walker. We must be getting close.'

Desmond McGrath

One Hundred and Twelve

F BI, CIA, it didn't matter. They were scared.

Someone had slipped unnoticed up to their camp and silently and professionally taken one of them out and disappeared without trace.

Only a pro could do that.

That made them even more scared.

'And he's got his gun too,' said Al Gordino.

'He probably had one anyway,' said Frank Klugman. 'Just didn't need to use it.'

'I don't fucking like this,' confessed Todd Chandler. 'I'm starting to feel more like the hunted than the hunter.'

'Tell me about it,' Al Gordino said. 'I'm all for

fucking off back. Who gives a shit about Caviar?'

Frank Klugman put it in a nutshell. 'I couldn't give a flying fuck about Caviar either. I'm just here for the money. What we've got to figure out is how far we are prepared to go for it.'

'Yeah,' said Todd Chandler. 'That's the bottom line of it.'

'Well, one more slit throat and I'm outa here,' declared Al Gordino. 'Yeah, as long as it's not yours,' said Todd Chandler.

One Hundred and Thirteen

Caviar hadn't struggled.

David Walker untied her.

'So?' asked Caviar.

'There's one less of them,' David Walker answered her coldly.

'Who killed him?' asked Caviar. 'You or the madman?'

'Me, this time. Survival. Needs must. They're hunting me. They know the score.'

Something like admiration stirred in Caviar. Whatever else he was, David Walker was a man. A real man. She knew it wasn't normal but she lusted for him.

She obviously didn't love him. But he did something to her.

He made her want.

Want him.

To fuck him.

To fuck his brains out.

'I want you, David,' she said. 'Now.'

Still aroused from the adrenalin of the kill, he dragged her roughly into his arms and buried his mouth into hers with an animal passion.

They didn't undress.

They just tore the clothes from one another until they were both naked.

Like two randy dogs they fought to please one another.

Nothing was too much trouble.

Nothing!

With gusto they licked and sucked and fucked. For what must have been hours they sweated, groaned and cried out several times until they were finally exhausted and spent out.

David Walker collapsed off Caviar, pulling himself out of her, and lay on his back by the stream.

Caviar wasn't dead. She just looked it.

'David, that was the best sex ever. It can never be better than that.'

'Oh yes it can. Trust me.'

One Hundred and Fourteen

It was cold at night in the hills.

Todd Chandler pulled his blanket round his shoulders and moved as close as he could to the campfire.

They were camped at the bottom of the stream. The third stream. The last stream. Tomorrow they would trace it to its source at the top of the hills and hopefully get a clue to the whereabouts of Caviar.

But there was an air of doom and gloom about the place.

The commitment was gone.

They had been four retired FBI and CIA agents.

Now they were three.

Did they really need this?

Doubt heaped upon doubt.

To be honest. they hadn't got the balls for it any more.

Although they didn't want to admit it.

They were scared.

They were vulnerable.

Drinking heavily that night, they made the decision to quit in the morning.

Who needs money when they're dead?

They decided to go home tomorrow.

All but one: Frank Klugman.

He didn't see David Walker as he slithered up to him in his sleep.

He just felt himself jerk as a hand to the mouth silenced him and the knife slid easily under his ribcage to rupture his heart with a vicious twist.

As silently as he came, David Walker left.

As the sun rose up for breakfast there was

panic in the camp.

No!

You could call it terror.

Desmond McGrath

One Hundred and Fifteen

Finn McCooll found the second body at midday.

Expertly examining the area for tracks, he decided that the two remaining pairs of feet had taken to their car and cleared off the way they had come.

And he didn't blame them.

'50 percent casualty rate, I make it,' he said. 'Not good.'

I knew first-hand how deadly David Walker could be.

No matter what you did, you could never seem to stop him.

I felt my blood run cold.

It was Liam Dooly who spoke first. 'I think we should all split up. Go solo. He's picked them off one at a time. He'll do the same to us. It won't be so easy if we're scattered. Not too far. But far enough to watch each other's backs.'

'Good idea,' I said. 'We'll spread out and sleep two at a time while the other two stay alert.'

I stayed in the camp and built up the campfire. It got cold at night in the hills. I unscrewed the top off a cheap Rioja red wine and drank it from the bottle.

Common, I know.

But there you go!

I thought of Caviar.

Was she safe?

Was she even alive?

I could only hope.

I tipped a tin of sausage and beans into a small saucepan and stirred it over the fire.

It was disgusting.

I made up my mind that in the morning I was going to hunt down a rabbit.

I looked at the time.

It was nearly eight o'clock. I didn't want to miss the news, so I jumped up with my saucepan of shit and a spoon and sat in the car with the radio on.

What I heard shocked me.

It was a radio summary of an earlier in-depth *Sky News* report.

Desmond McGrath

One Hundred and Sixteen

Eight o'clock *Sky News*.

Peter Philips stood before the cameras shuffling his papers.

'Things took another dramatic turn today in the hunt for missing rock star Caviar. Of the four men, all ex-FBI and CIA agents, sent to find her, only two returned.

'What can you tell us Emma?'

Emma Griffiths spoke into her mike.

'Yes, Peter, I can confirm that only two agents returned - and may I say, Philip, in a state of shock. If their account of what happened turns out to be true, then police can expect to find two bodies.

'One with his throat cut. The other killed commando-style with a knife under the rib cage into the heart. And who is responsible? That is the big question. According to all sources, the agents were tracking - wait for it - Jack Reec!

'Yes, Peter, more mystery surrounds this man. People just seem to disappear or die everywhere he goes.'

'Yes, Emma,' said Peter Philips. 'Can you tell us if there's a definite link between Reec and the killings?'

'I can tell you that there seems to be no other. Except, of course, if you believe Reec and his murdering IRA friends, that there's a mystery serial killer on the loose in Spain. A theory that has yet to be proved. And frankly one that many doubt! Baloney, I say.

'It seems to most that the likely villains in the disappearance of Caviar are Jack Reec, Liam Dooly, William Dufacy and Joseph Cahill. Yet still no ransom has been demanded.

'The mystery just seems to thicken. Thank you, Philip. This is Emma Griffiths handing you back to the studio from the Costa del Sol, Spain.'

'Thank you, Emma.'

One Hundred and Seventeen

I couldn't believe it.

There and then I decided I had to go back in the morning and set the record straight.

I just hoped they would believe me.

I filled in the Irishmen at breakfast.

'I've a feeling we're getting close,' said Dooly. 'Me and the boys will keep going. Finn here will find him soon if he's out here. You go back and set things straight. The boys back home won't be too happy, either,' he added. 'Not the best of publicity.'

'Specially not with the Real IRA kicking off again,' said Joe Cahill. 'They've claimed responsibility for the two Brit soldiers, but they won't want to be blamed for Caviar.'

'Yes, bad news for them,' interjected Billy Dufacy. 'I think you'd best try and set things straight, Jack.'

'Hello Paddy,' said Finn McCooll. 'I have a thought.'

'Share it then,' said Dufacy.

'It don't need *three* of us to go scouting. If I was to go on alone it would be a lot less noisy and far safer. If youse two cook the dinner I'll do a little quiet reccie and see what I can find. No need for us all to go. I can have a little nose around and make a report this evening.'

'Makes sense,' I said. 'I'll go and try to get back in the morning, tomorrow.'

Everyone murmured in agreement, and I set off.

I made a call on my cell.

Delicious Fantastico took it.

'For sure, Jack,' she said. 'I can't wait.'

Maybe I wouldn't be back too early in the morning!

One Hundred and Eighteen

Caviar was sucking David Walker off.

He'd bathed in the stream and she was enjoying it too. She didn't feel like sex again herself. The morning session was enough for her.

But she knew that the best hope of escape and survival was through his cock.

And she was no stranger!

Someone had once asked her 'What's the difference between liking and loving?'

'Swallowing it or spitting it out,' was the answer.

She spat it out.

David Walker didn't care either way.

'So how am I doing?' she asked him.

'Just fine.'

'So do you still think you'll kill me?'

'Coin's in the air.'

'Thanks.'

'But you're doing good.'

'I'll just have to try and keep it up, then,' she winked mischievously as she licked him again.

'You just do that small thing.' David Walker grinned back at her.

'Not so small,' Caviar said flicking it with her finger. 'If the worst comes to the worst, will you kill me on the job?'

'You can bet on that,' said David Walker. 'I always do.'

Suddenly it didn't seem so funny any more to Caviar.

One Hundred and Nineteen

Finn McCooll was sure that he hadn't been spotted.

He had!

And little did he know it, but soon he was going to say 'Hello' to Paddy for the last time...

Whoever *he* was.

David Walker waited.

It was never going to be a contest.

As I was making love to Delicious Fantastico, Finn McCooll was being violently murdered.

What was it with me?

Just being around me seemed to be the kiss

of death.

It was like a curse.

But it never touched me.

Just everyone around me.

It was as if I breezed through life like a soft wind, but behind me followed a tornado.

Why?

I don't know.

But I would eventually find out that when Finn McCooll didn't make his report that evening, Liam Dooly and Bill and Joe went looking for him.

And when they found the poor butchered bastard they swore a terrible vengeance.

On David Walker.

I doubted they could pull it off.

We're talking David Walker.

One Hundred and Twenty

I went straight to Police Headquarters.

When they heard I was there, a media frenzy erupted. The police station was under siege. vans with aerials, TV crews and cameras, hordes of photographers.

News crews chattered in every conceivable language into the microphones as they looked into cameras. A *Sky News* helicopter hovered overhead, causing a severe downdraft that was tormenting those crews beneath it.

Inside the interview room I was grilled relentlessly and mercilessly for eight hours solid by four hard and aggressive Spanish detectives.

Question after question.

Accusation after accusation.

Finally I managed to convince them that I had nothing to do with the two murdered agents.

Caviar had been kidnapped by David Walker, and I believed her to be alive. If not safe.

The Irishmen were hunting for her with the help of an expert tracker, and I believed that we were the best chance of getting her back alive.

I'm sure that if it wasn't for the media pressure they would have been quite happy to go with that.

But the world was watching, and I knew they were going to do something.

And I just got the feeling it was going to be a major fuck-up.

They just didn't have a clue.

They sneaked me out the back, more for their sake than mine, to escape the mob.

I fled to the welcoming arms of Delicious Fantastico.

In the morning I took the call from Dooly.

'He's killed Finn McCooll,' he told me solemnly, 'with a knife. Just like the others.'

'I'm on my way,' I said.

Desmond McGrath

One Hundred and Twenty-one

Peter Philips broke into the programme. 'We bring you a newsflash on the disappearance of rock star Caviar. What can you tell us, Emma?'

'Yes, Peter,' said Emma Griffiths as she flashed onto the screen worldwide. 'There have been more dramatic developments here. The Chief of Police has just emerged from Headquarters and issued a carefully worded statement. Briefly, Peter, it said that Jack Reec had voluntarily come into the police station with vital information on the disappearance of Caviar. He cannot divulge that information as it is part of an ongoing enquiry. But he did say that as a result of this information Jack Reec and his Irish counterparts have been eliminated as suspects in the disappearance. Ongoing police operations are to follow, and a manhunt to be mounted for the new suspect, as yet unnamed. When asked about the present whereabouts of Jack Reec, he would only say he has been released without charge.

'But where, Peter? With half the world watching, he disappeared back into thin air and what does all this mean to the fate of Caviar?

'What part is Jack Reec playing in this game? Hero or villain? Who knows? Will we ever know? The mystery deepens. Watch this space.

'Emma Griffiths, handing back to the studios from the Costa del Sol.'

One Hundred and Twenty-two

'So what is it with you and Jack?' asked Caviar. 'You owe me that, if I'm going to die.'

'I do, you're right,' said David Walker thoughtfully. 'It's a long story.'

'I'm going nowhere.'

'True.'

'So?'

'The other one,' he began. 'The one in my head. Butchered and killed his girlfriend. Took her for a magnificent meal and a romantic walk along a moonlit beach, then raped her and cut her up and floated her body out to sea.'

'So he was sore at you,' said Caviar.

David Walker smiled at her irony. 'You could say that. Tried to hunt me down with his friends. Followed me all the way across Spain and Morocco.'

'And?'

'I had to kill them.' I could have killed Jack, but I spared him for another day.'

Caviar remembered.

'Shot him three times.'

'Correct.'

'Once in each shoulder and once in the leg. Why?'

'He was a worthy adversary. Deserved another chance. Now he'll come and try to save you.'

'So this is a game.'

'Exactly.'

'So my life doesn't mean a rat's ass to you, you just want to play against Jack Reec.'

'That's about it.'

'Great! So that's why there's no ransom demand,' Caviar said.

'Don't need the money; just complicate things,' David Walker told her.

'So really I've got no fucking chance?' said Caviar, as it all began to dawn on her.

'Not unless Jack comes to save you.'

One Hundred and Twenty-three

Suddenly Caviar felt very alone.

Vulnerable.

In danger.

Scared.

Frightened.

In fear of her life.

Fucking terrified.

'Please say you won't kill me,' she said shakily.

'To be truthful,' he answered her, 'I don't want to. But if it comes to it I won't be able to stop myself.'

'Then let me go then,' she pleaded. 'Now.'

'Can't do that,' David Walker shrugged. 'Doesn't work like that.'

'But why?'

'Don't know. Can't tell you. That's how it happens.'

'What happens?'

'Someone else takes over,' he explained. 'And then it's not me. I won't be the one that kills you.'

'So how do I talk to this other guy?' Caviar asked.

'You can't. He lives in my head.'

David Walker was getting agitated.

'You mean you've no control over him?' said Caviar.

'Just shut the fuck up, will you!' he screamed at her. 'Do you think I want this? Enjoy this? I fucking hate this, but there's nothing I can do about it when it starts.'

His head fell into his hands and he started to sob.

Quietly.

Gently.

Caviar reached out to him. She took him in her arms and held him tenderly.

She almost felt sorry for him.

She felt his warm salty tears on her face and tongue as her eyes darted wildly around, searching for the gun.

One Hundred and Twenty-four

The assault force had been assembled.

Forty special forces personnel.

Twenty on the ground and twenty in the helicopter. Armed to the teeth and ready to go.

I feared the worst.

It all seemed a bit Mickey Mouse. Not thought through. Just not planned enough. There were enough of them. Don't get me wrong, but I just didn't think they knew what they were getting into.

Strength in numbers could sometimes work, but I still thought a small quiet team could do it better.

But having said that, Todd Chandler and his

CIA/FBI men couldn't do it.

And then there was Finn McCooll.

Maybe I was wrong.

Anyway, the land forces set off first in their jeeps while the airborne forces stood ready for the call.

Based on my information and that of the late Finn McCooll, they surrounded the area most likely to be the Rabbit Man's hiding place.

Of course, David Walker spotted them a mile off.

'I'm taking you higher,' he told Caviar. 'I'll have to hide you for a while. There's work to be done.'

He took her by the hand and led her up the mountain to the top of the stream. Caviar was breathless and exhausted when they got there. There was a small hidden outcrop of rock with good shade that he decided to keep her in.

'I'll have to tie you,' he told her.

'But what if you don't make it back?' she asked with concern.

'You better hope I do,' he said as he started to bind her wrists and ankles expertly.

More out of despair than sentiment she said, 'Good luck.'

'Thanks,' he said and took off.

He planned to outmanoeuvre them. He only had one handgun. He needed better weapons. If he could pick one of them off he could be better armed.

Even the odds more.

He saw the one. Slower than the rest.

Maybe just unfit or maybe a little more cautious.

Or scared.

Either way, it was a big mistake.

Fatal.

Like a cat stalking a bird, he crept up slowly behind the soldier and pounced.

Left hand over his mouth, he cut his throat cleanly and lowered him quietly to the ground.

David Walker stripped the body and then himself. In minutes he was dressed in the Spanish forces uniform and flak jacket, and armed with an AK47 assault rifle and six hand grenades. Donning the dead man's cap, he smiled to himself.

He bet he looked great.

To get an adrenalin rush, he promised himself that he was going to fuck Caviar that night in the uniform.

He knew he'd love it, and she would, for sure. He was fired up. High octane. Go go go!

One Hundred and Twenty-five

David Walker waved back to the man ahead of him as he was called forward and told, he guessed, to get a move on.

He quickened his pace in order catch up.

He could see most of the group spread out in a circle and closing in on the stream by his camp.

As soon as he reached the man in front he shot him straight through the forehead as he turned to greet him. The bullet smashed out of the back of his head leaving a gaping hole. Red and white matter spattered all around as he spun and crashed to a sprawling heap at David Walker's feet.

The echo of the shot resounded around the hills. Birds took to flight and every other soldier turned in its direction.

David Walker frantically waved to them to get down. He ran at a crouch towards the nearest two.

He blasted them to death with a deadly burst of fire from the AK47. There was panic and confusion. Someone called for the air support.

Not bothering to reload, David Walker snatched up the two men's rifles and raced ahead to the confused, poorly trained Spanish force.

They were running now towards each other, closing the circle, watching their charging comrade shouting and waving his arms as if in warning.

But now he was firing at them and they were falling.

And then the chopper swooped in overhead. It hovered, side wide open, troops ready to jump out. David Walker ran towards it, shouting and waving. It was settling to land at about thirty feet.

Almost in slow motion, they watched as the first grenade floated over their heads into the aircraft.

Followed immediately by the second.

The first exploded, showering bodies, dead and alive, out of the doors onto the ground. The chopper lurched in the throes of death, rising first and then almost flipping over. When the second grenade went off, it disintegrated in a violent ear-shattering fireball.

David Walker threw himself to the ground for cover as burning fuel and wreckage crashed all around him.

There were screams from the dying but most were already dead.

David Walker could have killed the remainder of the ground force.

But he spared them. To tell the story.

One Hundred and Twenty-six

I listened to it on *Sky News.*

'This is a newsflash,' announced Peter Philips. 'News is coming in of a failed attempt by Spanish special forces to rescue international singing sensation Caviar. What can you tell us, Emma?'

'Yes indeed, Peter,' said Emma Griffiths into her mic. 'It seems there has been a disastrous failed attempt to rescue Caviar. Massive casualties Peter. Forty troops began the mission. Five returned. Thirty-five dead, no wounded. Plus the two crew of the helicopter. Thirty-seven Spanish dead in all. Truly a shocking statistic, Peter. The biggest single loss in Spanish troops since the Civil War. What army, you may ask, could deal such a crushing blow? It seems just one man.'

'Incredible,' interrupted Peter Philips.

'Yes, Peter,' replied Emma Griffiths. 'A humiliating defeat for the special forces.'

'But Emma, you say just one man. How can you be so sure? It seems too incredible.'

'That one man it is emerging Peter is David Walker, a highly trained and dangerous British former SAS officer. Hopes are fading rapidly for the safe return of Caviar. Reluctantly, all eyes are now turning to Jack Reec, the original suspect in the kidnapping. He is the only man who knows David Walker, albeit to his cost. The only man who could even identify him. But will he even want to help? Will he want to risk his life? Only time will tell Peter. This is Emma Griffiths, handing you back to the studios.'

I leaned back in my sunlounger and took a long drink of my vodka and tonic.

My cell phone rang.

'Hello Jack.'

It was David Walker.

One Hundred and Twenty-seven

'You should have warned them, Jack,' he said. 'It wasn't a fair fight. They had no chance.'

'What do you want?' I asked him.

'An equal opponent, Jack,' he told me. 'You.'

'But why?' I asked. 'You've beaten me once. What's the point?'

'A rematch, Jack. Winner takes all. To the victor go the spoils. You win, Jack, and Caviar goes free. I give you my word. I won't hurt a hair on her head.'

'And if I don't?'

'She's mine.'

'But what for?'

'To use and abuse as I see fit. For as long as I like.'

I shuddered at the thought. And also at the thought of going up against David Walker again.

'Speak to her, Jack.'

The voice of Caviar cried out over the phone. 'Come for me, Jack! Please. You're my only hope,' she pleaded.

'I will,' I told her, 'be strong.'

David Walker took over.

'Very touching, that, Jack. I'm sure you'll do your best. Let's not hope it's good enough.'

'What kind of animal are you?' I asked him.

'The worst kind. The kind you meet in your worst nightmares.'

I couldn't argue with that. I'd met him once before.

And it was a nightmare.

'Bring the Irishmen too, Jack. They're good for a little side entertainment.'

I didn't answer to that.

'Must go now, Jack. Feeling a little horny. What a superstar! Puts on a fabulous show. But I suspect you know that anyway.'

I didn't.

'Happy days.'

The phone went dead.

One Hundred and Twenty-eight

'A little side entertainment,' spat Liam Dooly, feathers flying. 'The little flucking gobshite. Where I come from, they'd keep him as a pet.'

'Don't be so sure, Liam,' I told him. 'Many of my friends made that mistake to their cost. Look at Finn McCooll.'

'Finn McCoule was a danger to no man,' Dooly shot back. 'He was a hunter, a tracker, a sniffer dog. Not a killer or a warrior.'

'Well, he's dead, and so are the two Yanks and thirty seven Spanish Special Forces. That makes forty in all.'

Billy Dufacy and Joe Cahill hadn't said a word up to now. We were sitting by the pool at the farm, bathing in soft moonlight from a full moon, drinking San Miguel from the bottle.

'Jack's right,' said Cahill. 'Walker's no thick eejit. He's smart. He's trying to fuck with us. Get us to be careless. Wants us to fire up and go after him in a rage so he can take us out. The only way we can get him is if we stay cool. Outmanoeuvre him.'

'I'll go with that,' agreed Billy Dufacy. 'He always seems to know everyone's position. Then he quietly picks them off. We have to move like mice. Only at night. We sleep and stay under cover in the day. Become invisible.'

'Sounds like a plan,' I said.

But David Walker had read their thoughts and had a plan of his own.

Keeping his promise to himself, he had the greatest sex with Caviar in his new Spanish forces uniform, then broke camp. He packed up the car with what he wanted and prepared to move on in the morning.

Later he made love again to Caviar on the rock in the stream. She just couldn't get enough. Could she?

One Hundred and Twenty-nine

'All but the most optimistic have now given up all hope of finding rock star Caviar alive,' announced Emma Griffiths. 'With the death toll now standing at forty, it seems that Jack Reec and his IRA friends are reluctant to join the hunt. And who could blame them? With no ransom being demanded, it can only be concluded that the motive for abduction is sexual. Poor Caviar. With the world at her feet, such a tragic waste. This is Emma Griffiths handing you back to the studios.'

Caviar listened to the repeated broadcast on the car radio as they travelled. 'Where are we going?' she asked.

'Don't know yet,' said David Walker, 'but away from here. I need to put some space between us. If Jack does decide to come for you he'll waste a few days crashing around in the hills. By then we can be far away. Like it?'

'Yeah. Great plan.'

But the truth was that a plan was forming in David Walker's head.

Jerez de la Frontera to the west on the Costa de la Luz. There was an airport there. A small one.

Jerez Main five kilometers north of the city.

Not that he was intending to buy a ticket.

It would be a few hours' drive. He told Caviar. She said she would take a nap. David Walker was glad of that. It would give him peace. Time to think.

Time to plan the next move.

With no satnav or map he was driving from memory.

Following the sparse road signs he knew he was going in the right direction. The closer he got the better would be the signs.

Darkness was closing in.

The road signs became more frequent.

Then a plane on the sign: Aeropuerto.

It was dark now and Caviar was grunting in her sleep. Tossing restlessly in her seat belt. Straining against it, as if dreaming badly.

David Walker ignored her and cruised to a stop at the perimeter wire of the airfield. The usual airport lights were on. Runway lights and high pylons, with various building lights in the distance.

He found himself at the end of the runway. A small jet careered down it towards him and screamed off over his head.

He loved planes and airports, had done since he was a kid. He sat in the car, gazing down the runway, mesmerised by the two rows of lights and the headlights of the next plane as it screamed towards him. Then, at seemingly the last second before crashing into him, it lifted off into the sky for some distant destination.

Before she knew what was happening, he had tied Caviar's right wrist to his left, giving her about three feet of line. As she sleepily protested he pulled her from the car.

'Keep it quiet,' he told her. 'don't utter a sound. Your life depends on it.'

'Where are we?' she asked confused.

'No matter. Just follow me.'

'Do I have a choice?' she asked raising her roped wrist.

'Good point. No.'

'Roger that, then,' she said almost sarcastically.

'We need to get onto the airfield,' he told her, ignoring what she said.

'They have an entrance.'

'Sure they do,' He smirked. 'But I find it rather dull and boring.'

'And too public?'

'That too.'

'So what are...?'

'Just shut the fuck up and keep your gob shut!'

'Gob?'

'Mouth.'

He gave her a backhand across it for effect.

It worked.

There was always a breach in every defence. All you had to do was find it. Crouching low, he towed Caviar behind him along the wire.

And there it was. A breach.

Damage to the fence that was obviously recent and yet unrepaired. This was Spain, after all. Widening the hole in the wire David Walker pushed Caviar through and crawled into the airfield behind her.

The hangars.

That's what he was looking for. He saw them far ahead to his right, past the beginning of the runway.

That's where they were going.

One Hundred and Thirty

The hangar seemed vast to David Walker. But of course by comparison it was only small. There was a scattering of small planes, Cessnas and Lear Jets.

Crews and mechanics smoked and talked as they passed the time away in idle banter. It could be a long night.

Just on standby.

With Caviar tethered to him by just three feet of rope, David Walker assessed the situation and the most likely object for his needs.

'That Lear Jet,' he said to Caviar, pointing. 'It looks like it's prepared for passengers.'

'I see it. So?'

'We're passengers.'

To David Walker it appeared that the last minute checks were being done. The pilot was in the cockpit with earphones, speaking to the engineers on the ground. An engine revved and a thumb went up. Another engine whined and another thumb went up from the cockpit this time.

Ladders were against the door. David Walker watched like a cat waiting to pounce on a mouse. He only had one chance or the mouse would get away. He was close to the aircraft now. He tugged Caviar. She jerked forward.

He watched the pilot in the cockpit. He was busy checking his instruments. The engineers were moving away from the jet. There was a small window of opportunity. David Walker tugged Caviar, and together they ran forward to the plane and up the ladder inside. They dived to the right and hid in the seats.

They breathed heavily for a minute then heard the steps being withdrawn and the plane moving slowly forward.

They were onboard.

One Hundred and Thirty-one

Buenas noches, amigo!' said David Walker to the pilot as he held the gun to his temple. 'Are we ready for take-off?'

'Señor, I do not understand.'

'Then let me explain,' David Walker told him in his most serious tone. 'Are we fuelled?'

'Sí señor.'

'Then we can take off?'

'No, señor. It is impossible.'

'How so?'

'We have no clearance, señor.'

'I'll take responsibility.'

'Señor, it cannot be done. I need permission from Air Traffic Control. I cannot just take off. I need to log a flight plan. A destination. I need a take-off slot. Clearance.'

David Walker forced the barrel of the gun against the pilot's head until it hurt.

'Listen to me, amigo. If you want to live the rest of your life peacefully with your family then you had better do exactly what I say. Trust me, I am a desperate man. I am trying to escape. To survive. Together we can both survive. Now fly this fucking plane down the runway and get us out of here.'

'To where, señor?'

'I don't know yet. Just out of here.'

'You better secure the door señor or we will all be flying but without the plane.'

'Good point,' said David Walker. 'Roger that.' He dragged in the door and slammed it closed.

'Let's go.'

Within seconds the Lear Jet was bouncing along the runway, gaining speed rapidly then lurching skywards into the dark night.

David Walker sat behind the pilot. 'Well done, amigo!'

'So where to, señor?' he asked.

David Walker didn't know but he had to make a decision. From nowhere he just said, 'Turkey.'

'Copy that señor.'

And so, with a turn of the controls, the plane veered towards Turkey.

One Hundred and Thirty-two

'Amigo, I know that you are a desperate man,' said the pilot. 'But if I cooperate with you will you spare me? I have a wife and two bambinos. It is all I ask.'

'You have my word, amigo,' said David Walker genuinely. 'I have no wish to harm you. I have no need. Take me to my destination and you are free.'

'*Gracias*, señor,' the pilot thanked him. 'For that I am grateful. But if you wish to remain anonymous we will have to fly low. Below the radar. It is dangerous.'

'Can you do it?'

'Oh yes señor. I have done it many times before.'

'Really,' said David Walker with a touch of admiration. 'Then let's do it.'

'Sí, señor, let's go.'

Skimming hills and trees, the pilot expertly sped over all sorts of uncharted terrain.

David Walker was in awe with admiration.

'Where did you learn to do that?' he asked.

'The Military, señor,' he replied. 'Low flying exercises.'

'You learned well,' Walker told him.

'Thank you, señor,' said the pilot proudly. 'Where in Turkey do you want me to land?'

'No idea,' said David Walker. 'Never been there. How long does it take?'

'Who knows?' the pilot shrugged. 'Two hours, four hours, six hours... How far do you want to go? It's a big place.'

'Somewhere quiet, in the middle of nowhere,' David Walker told him.

'But señor there are no airfields in the middle of nowhere. How am I supposed to land?'

'I'm sure you'll figure it out,' said David

Walker, 'somewhere hard and flat, I should imagine. When we get there, keep your eyes peeled for somewhere to land.'

'But señor...'

David Walker poked the gun to his head.

'Sí, señor, I understand.'

One Hundred and Thirty-three

As they zigzagged, crossed and turned, rose and fell beneath the radar, undiscovered, David Walker spotted a possible landing site in a valley with a river and lush green trees on the surrounding hills.

It was miles from anywhere. Just what he was looking for.

'Take her down,' he told the pilot. 'Down there.'

'But señor it is impossible,' he said. 'There is nowhere to land.'

'I'm sure you can find a place.'

'But señor surely you do not want to die in a plane crash?'

'I sure don't,' agreed David Walker, 'but I'm equally sure that you don't want to either. So let's get this plane safely on the fucking ground.'

With no other option left, the pilot scoured the area for hope. He found it in the shape of what appeared to be a dried up riverbed. Long, flat but bumpy.

Resigned to what had to be done, the pilot went into the zone.

The calm zone.

The professional zone.

Training took over.

'Speak no more, señor. I want to hear no more of your words. Be quiet.'

Focussing on exactly what had to be done, the pilot chose his time and spot and with excellent skill homed in on his chosen landing place. As he wrestled the controls, the plane veered from side to side. The wings flipped up and down from left to right.

He steadied the plane.

It rocked and rolled from left to right and up and down, then bounced precariously on the bumpy, dried up riverbed. Pounding headlong to disaster, it finally stopped, just a few feet short of a monstrous 400-year-old tree.

All three on board breathed a massive sigh of relief.

Sparing any pain and anguish for the pilot, David Walker shot him in the back of his head.

He hated breaking his word but he had no choice.

It had to be done.

'Why did you do that?' asked Caviar, not shocked.

'Had to be done,' he said matter-of-factly. 'Now there are only two people in the world that know where we are. Me and you.'

'And where's that?'

David Walker stifled a laugh and chuckled.

'Fuck knows.'

Desmond McGrath

One Hundred and Thirty-four

'So what now?' asked Caviar.

'We bury the pilot before he starts to draw flies,' David Walker answered. 'We'll drag him well away from the plane and cover him in rocks. We haven't got a shovel, and I hate digging anyway.

'OK so then what?' Caviar asked again.

'We turn this plane into a home,' he told her. 'We have everything here we need. It's like the biggest camper van in the world. I'll reconnoitre the area and see what we can expect to live on. Source the food and water supply. When I've seen to the pilot, we can check all we have on board. It was prepared for flight so there must be food and drink aplenty for the short term. We can make it our home for a while until I decide what to do next.'

'Great,' grunted Caviar.

'Take off your clothes,' said David Walker.

'What!'

'Take off your clothes,' he answered as he began taking off his.

'Why?'

'Because this is freedom,' he told her. 'The ultimate freedom. We are here in the most beautiful place, miles from anywhere, alone. We don't need clothes. It's warm and sunny. We have our home and the most beautiful vast garden in the world. We are alone. We have freedom. We don't need clothes. Take them off. Be free.'

Caviar thought about it.

'That's cool man. Really cool. Let's get it on.'

She stripped naked and threw her arms in the air, scattering her clothes.

'Freedom. Let's drink to it.'

David Walker found some booze and they got drunk.

Then they had the greatest sex and he fell asleep.

Never mind the flies; the pilot would have to wait until tomorrow.

One Hundred and Thirty-five

They sorted out the pilot first thing the next day.

'Don't run away, will you,' David Walker joked. 'I'm going for a look around. See what's out there.'

'Yeah, like I got some place to go,' scoffed Caviar.

The irony of it wasn't lost on David Walker. 'Well, you never know.'

'Yeah, sure, go get me something to eat.'

'OK.'

Turkey spans two continents, linking mainland Europe with Asia across the narrow straits of the Bosporus and Dardanelles.

European Turkey (Thrace), to the north of the Sea of Marmara, shares borders with Bulgaria and Greece. Asian Turkey, much of which is known as Anatolia or Asia Minor, is much larger in area and borders Syria and Iraq to the south and south east, Iran and Armenia to the east, and Georgia to the north east. The long coastlines are washed by the Black Sea to the north, the Aegean to the west and the Mediterranean to the south.

European Turkey is characterised by fertile rolling plains surrounded by low mountains. On the Asian side, Western Anatolia is crossed by long mountain ridges separated by deep valleys. South of the central Anatolian plateau, the three main ranges of the Taurus Mountains flank the Mediterranean coast. Farther east, a complex of even higher mountain ranges culminates in the massive cone of Mount Ararat. To the south west is Lake Van.

Thick, scrubby undergrowth characterises the Mediterranean south and west of the country. The Black Sea coast supports dense forest, while the drier interior is covered mainly in steppe grassland. Bears and red deer are still found in the forests, and colourful flocks of greater flamingos thrive on some of the lakes.

David Walker guessed from the flight time and landscape that he was somewhere in the middle of the European side between the Black Sea coast and the Mediterranean coast.

Well, wherever he was, he was loving it.

The forest was green and lush. That meant water. Lots of it. As he threaded his way through the undergrowth he could hear the warning calls of the animals and birds telling each other he was there. A cacophony of sounds rang in his ears as he happily strolled through his garden.

A red deer stood its ground ahead of him, snorting and spreading its nostrils, steam flowing from them. It stamped a warning. David Walker smiled. He could no more fly to the moon than harm such a beautiful animal.

'Have no fear,' he said to himself.

He felt the beast's acknowledgement as it relaxed and bobbed its head on its long red neck.

I have no fear of you, it told him back.

They respected each other and carelessly went their separate ways.

The smell of the forest was pungent, beautiful: damp leaves, dry earth, sweaty tree bark. David Walker could taste it, relish the flavours. Like a chef in a kitchen with his herbs and spices, this was his kitchen.

His domain.

What he was born for.

He knew there was water near. He could smell it. He could taste it. The plants and trees grew lusher, darker, greener. Lances of sunlight stroked between the trees as they began to open out into a clearing.

A massive clearing.

A clearing filled with water.

A lake.

The most beautiful lake he had ever seen.

He sat on the ground and wondered at it.

Oh my God he thought.

This truly must be the Garden of Eden.

He couldn't wait to show it to Caviar.

Part Three

Three Months Later

Somewhere in Turkey

One Hundred and Thirty-six

'This might sound ridiculous, David,' Caviar told him, 'but I've never been happier in my life.'

'Me too,' he replied truthfully.

'Do you still think you will kill me?' she asked.

'I never wanted to kill you,' he said. 'It's not me, it's the monster in my head. If anyone kills you it will be him. Not me. So don't worry.'

'Great!' said Caviar. 'And I can't believe I haven't worn a stitch of clothes for three months. It just feels so great.'

'You only need clothes to keep warm,' he said. 'The primitive tribes of the world have never been ashamed of their bodies. They

473

embrace them. It's only the so-called educated who have made our bodies a taboo. They created mystery that led to curiosity that then led to lust that eventually led to fear and rape.'

'Christ. How deep is that!' asked Caviar. She hadn't written a song for ages but she could feel the makings of one. In fact, over the past three months she had idled away the time writing her next album. The last few weeks she had been stuck.

Suddenly she was filled with inspiration.

'It just feels so good here, David,' she confessed. 'This has got to have been the greatest experience of my life.'

Indeed it had been.

After using the first couple of days to bury the pilot and adjust they had begun to turn the plane into a home. Using the plane's extensive toolkit they began stripping out the seats, leaving the back two rows by the galley for a seating area. Using the cushions they made a bed area. Surplus seats were deployed in the 'garden'.

Stripping unneeded electric wire, David Walker made snares to place all over the forest. Rabbits were plentiful. The lake provided ample fish and duck and the occasional goose. As much as he fancied a venison steak, David

Walker could not break his truce with the red deer.

It would be a total waste of an animal and meat.

But one day he came across an inquisitive stray goat. He shot it cleanly, and after skinning it and gutting it he fried the liver and boiled the heart with wild herbs and vegetables. Disjointing the best limbs for cooking, he sliced what he couldn't eat into thin strips and laid it on the wings of the plane in the sun to dry. Although it wouldn't taste great it was a good standby if things were tough or you were travelling. You could chew it dry or boil it up. It was emergency rationing.

He also dried fish to stockpile for a rainy day. He and Caviar spent endless days wandering the forest and swimming in the lake. It was midsummer and the weather was gorgeous. The stream that fed the lake from the mountains was an abundant source of trout. Fabulously tanned and healthy, David Walker and Caviar had an idyllic life.

How long could it last?

The plane's supplies of coffee, tea and drink had now run out. But it didn't seem to matter. It was a simple, uncomplicated, fulfilling life.

David Walker was a wonderful provider. He

had been trained to live off the land. Every expedition he took he came back with something. Wild mushrooms, wild roots and potatoes, even truffles. On this one occasion he came back with a particularly handsome fat duck. He tossed it to Caviar.

'Pluck that,' he said. 'Tonight we have wild duck and truffle sauce. You like?'

'I like,' laughed Caviar ripping into the feathers on the duck, down flying everywhere.

That night they took turns revolving the duck over the campfire. The stones David Walker had buried in the fire were white hot and the duck was spitting its fat onto them, intensifying the heat.

Crispy roast duck. The liver, heart and gizzard were simmering on the side in truffles and wild mushrooms.

From nowhere David Walker produced a bottle of red wine.

'I've been saving it,' he told Caviar, 'for a special occasion. And this is it.' It had a screw top, nothing fancy. He had two glasses and poured. 'To tomorrow,' he toasted.

'What happens tomorrow?' asked Caviar.

'We need to stock up on supplies,' he

answered. 'On one of my longer expeditions I came across a road. About ten miles from here. It's quiet and not much used, but it must go somewhere. Tomorrow I'm going to leave you. I probably won't be back that night or even the next day. Will you be alright?'

'I'm scared.'

'Don't be.'

'But out here alone...'

'You've been here three months, you know the country. You'll be safe,' he assured her. 'We need certain things. And above all I need my medication. It's run out.'

Caviar understood.

One Hundred and Thirty-seven

The first thing I thought of when I heard it on the news was David Walker.

A Lear Jet preparing to collect passengers, then suddenly taking off with no clearance and no flight plan! It was never kosher.

But it had totally disappeared. Vanished. Three months ago. It just had to have crashed. That was the only explanation.

It was three months and not a sign of it. If it hadn't crashed then it would have to have landed somewhere.

And it hadn't.

And if Walker and Caviar were on it they were dead.

I watched *Sky News.*

Emma Griffiths reported. 'Rock star Caviar has now been missing for almost four months without the slightest clue to her disappearance. It seems the world of rock has moved on, with a tribute release of her greatest hits. The phenomenon that was to be is now being compared to the legend that was John Lennon.

'What could there have been? What did she have left? Would she have been greater than Madonna, as some already think? The fact is that the world will never know. The phenomenon that was Caviar is gone. Emma Griffiths, handing you back to the studios.'

I couldn't believe that David Walker was dead. He was far too cunning a fox. And something told me Caviar was alive.

Don't ask me what.

The three Irishmen had become residents of the farm. Horny Formore and Delicious Fantistico had taken early retirement, much to Dooly's relief, and I have to admit to mine also.

I had a soft spot for 'Ice Cream' as I now called her.

But I wondered constantly about Caviar. How could the biggest star on the globe disappear without trace?

It was truly bizarre. And yet she had.

But as much as I pondered, I could get no answer, so I stuck it on the back-burner and decided to have a party.

Another one!

Desmond McGrath

One Hundred and Thirty-eight

At first light David Walker moved out. Dressed for the first time in three months, he felt strange.

His plan was to try and find a town and stock up supplies, then steal a car and get back to Caviar.

He knew she would be there.

There was nowhere to go.

And if he was honest, he missed her.

He wanted to get back to her.

With his medication.

So she would be safe.

He made good time through the forests. He knew it well. The road he sought was five miles beyond the lake. He was covering the ground fast. It was his territory. God help anyone who tried to take him out here.

He moved quickly and nimbly past the lake and beyond. A few miles to go. He was so fit he felt like a machine - a well-oiled machine.

He found himself on some high ground looking down on the road. A place he had been once before when he had found it. As before, there was no traffic.

He formed a plan.

And waited.

He saw the car in the distance.

God, it was old! He hadn't a clue what it was. A right knacker he thought to himself. He made his way down to the side of the road.

And waited.

It came towards him in a haze of blue smoke from its rear. David Walker crashed out of the trees and fell onto the road ahead of it as the knacker slammed on its dodgy brakes and tried to stop before it ran over him.

Thankfully, it did.

The Turkish peasant leapt from the car.

David Walker hadn't got a clue what he was saying, but gathered that he was either concerned for him or calling him a cunt. Either way he had stopped. That was the main thing.

After much gesticulating and sign language, David Walker was riding in the old knacker to somewhere.

Where?

He hadn't a clue.

But at least it was somewhere.

Desmond McGrath

One Hundred and Thirty-nine

Caviar was scared.

She felt vulnerable.

Alone.

Well, she was, you couldn't argue with that.

It sounded like a swarm of bees when she first heard it. A buzzing sound getting louder and louder. Coming from afar. But loud and getting louder. From out of the sun. Like in those old war films. The Japs coming out of the sun to blow you out of the sky.

It was a small light aircraft that swooped down through the valley out of the sun over her home.

Low. Intruding... on her space!

It turned and banked and flew down the valley again. As if that wasn't enough, it came back a third time.

Then flew off.

One Hundred and Forty

It was a one horse town wherever it was. David Walker was grateful for the lift.

He saw the thick red cross over the door and knew what it meant, Chemist or *Farmacia* or whatever it was in Turkey.

He entered the shop.

After a huge language struggle, he eventually emerged with three months' medication.

He was happy with that.

A good result.

He then went shopping.

Coffee, tea, sugar, long-life milk, beer, vodka, gin, bourbon, wine, port: you name it, he wanted it.

The trouble was, how was he getting it back?

It was at least a two-hour drive. On the side of the road he saw an old wreck of a car with a piece of cardboard with writing on it jammed between the windshield and the wipers. He guessed that it was a for sale sign in Greek.

He wasn't wrong. The instant he showed an interest in it a leather-faced old man appeared at this side. David Walker hadn't got a clue what he was saying but got some money out. It seemed to break down the language barrier. Eventually he became the proud owner of the biggest crock of shit he had ever seen in his life. He didn't even know what it was.

But it started and it ran. For how long, who knows? Hopefully for a few hours.

'RAC,' he said making a joke. The old man hadn't a clue what he had said but burst into fits of laughter as he slapped David Walker on the back and pocketed his money.

He couldn't believe his luck.

David Walker checked the fuel. Amazingly, there was half a tank, but to be certain he filled it up at the falling-down gas station on his way out of town.

It didn't have air con so he wound down the window. It stuck halfway. Oh well, at least he had some fresh air.

He found his landmark and drove his car as far into the trees as he could so that it was well concealed. He couldn't carry everything so he took what he could and most needed and started his hike through the forest.

He could collect the rest as he needed it. He was anxious to see Caviar, to make sure she was alright. He reached the lake and knew he was almost home. Completely relieved to see him, Caviar ran to him and jumped up into his arms.

They kissed.

Passionately.

'Oh David, I've been so scared out here on my own. I'm so glad you're back.'

'Me too. Let's have a drink. I've got some vodka.

'Fucking hell!' exclaimed Caviar. 'Vodka. Let's get it on. How many bottles?'

'Enough.'

They proceeded to get arseholed.

David Walker had bought two frozen chickens that were now defrosted; he lit the camp fire and hung them over it. With a carton of fresh orange juice, they began to demolish the vodka.

It was growing darker and the smells of the forest trees and earth mingled with the smell of roast chicken.

They finished the first bottle and cracked open the second. Naked again, like Caviar, David Walker felt free. Intoxicated, they were over each other like a rash. By the light and warmth of the campfire they climaxed together.

They rested a while then Caviar announced, 'I'm fucking starving.'

David Walker checked the chickens. 'The legs are done. The torsos will take longer. Cursing and burning his fingers, he pulled off the legs of both chickens and stuck them on a couple of plates. Ravenously tearing the hot flesh from the bones with their hands and teeth, they feasted.

'A small plane flew over today,' Caviar announced almost casually as she drank more vodka and orange. 'Must have flown over about three times.'

David Walker stopped eating. He poured more vodka into his orange. The alarm bells started to ring.

One Hundred and Forty-one

We were watching Sky News as we always did, Liam, myself, Dufacy and Cahill.

We had sent the women home. We wanted some lads' time. It could get a little claustrophobic at times. It was one of those chilly evenings when you wanted to be inside. We sat in front of the TV listening to Peter Philips. He was concluding with a small news item just coming in.

'Reports are coming from Turkey that a light aircraft on a pleasure flight has reported sighting a Lear Jet apparently parked in a clearing in the middle of a forest. According to the pilot, it appears to be undamaged. But what it is doing there one can only guess. Bizarre. But an old news story springs to mind that three months or so ago a Lear Jet took off from

Jerez Main on the Costa de la Luz without clearance or a flight plan. It was never seen again. Intriguing. We'll keep you fully updated with the story as it unfolds. Concluding *Sky News* for now, we'll be back with more updates at ten.'

'Are you thinking what I'm thinking?' Liam Dooly asked me.

'I'm thinking David Walker and Caviar,' I answered. 'That's what I'm thinking.'

'He's a slippery little eel, that one,' said Dooly. 'Got his name written all over it.'

'So what do you reckon?' Joe Cahill asked.

'I think it's watch this space, then Turkey - here we come!'

One Hundred and Forty-two

It was time to break camp. Abandon ship.

They were both desperately sad. It had been their home for over three months and they'd loved it.

But they had to leave it behind. With all the fond memories.

David Walker knew that it wouldn't be long before investigators were crawling all over the camp, seeking the story behind the Lear Jet in the forest.

Anyway, it was time to move on. 'Where are we going?' asked Caviar.

'No idea,' David Walker replied honestly. 'But there's a one-horse town a couple of hours drive from here. We'll go there first and get kitted out in some local garb.'

'Local garb?'

'Clothes. I need you to look totally inconspicuous.'

'Why don't you just let me go, David?' she asked him.

'I don't really know anymore,' he told her. 'Maybe I just like having you around. I like you. You're good fun to be with. I might even love you. And you're a great fuck too. What more can I say?'

'That kinda does it, I suppose,' Caviar shrugged. 'So, we getting married or what?'

David Walker had to laugh.

'Your funeral.'

'Yeah. That's what I'm afraid of.'

One Hundred and Forty-three

'I'm sorry to break into your programme, but this is an important news flash,' Peter Philips announced excitedly. 'Forensic investigators exploring the missing Lear Jet discovered in the depths of a forest in Turkey can say with absolute certainty that fingerprint evidence at the scene confirms without any doubt that the missing rock star phenomenon Caviar was on the plane.

'Sensational news. Caviar has been missing, presumed dead, for over three months, but evidence at the plane's campsite indicates that she was there as recently as a couple of days ago. What is going on?

As the whole world looks on, the renewed hunt for Caviar has reached an unprecedented intensity. Now there is true belief that she is still alive. And of course the rumours abound. Is it a giant publicity stunt? No, cry her managers. Has she suffered some breakdown and dropped out? Was she kidnapped, as first thought? If so, why no ransom demand? We'll know more shortly when our roving reporter Emma Griffiths arrives in Turkey. Your interrupted programme continues. I'm Peter Philips. Thank you.'

'Well, that settles it,' I said to the three Irishmen. 'We'd better get packed.'

One Hundred and Forty-four

Her hair was longer.

She was deep golden brown.

She looked older.

Not old.

Just older.

A woman.

Not a girl any more.

In three months she had matured in beauty.

Caviar bought some cheap local clothes in the one-horse-town and looked like a local.

It seems like a lifetime ago that she was a

huge global rock star.

The months of living outdoors and sleeping under the stars and the simplicity of her life had changed her.

And you know?

She liked it.

She liked the new Caviar.

And she even liked David Walker.

Inexplicably, perhaps.

But dare she say it?

She might even love him!

Or was it just survival?

She didn't know.

The beat-up wreck of an old car, whatever it was, was still running. David Walker was nursing it gently towards the Black Sea coast.

He hoped it would make it.

It did...

Just.

Part Four

The Black Sea

One Hundred and Forty-five

Technically, the Black Sea holiday resorts begin just outside Istanbul, but there are long stretches worth ignoring.

David Walker did.

The first unmissable stop is the city of Safranbolu, where some 800 of the finest nineteenth century Ottoman houses in Turkey have been beautifully restored, many as *pansiyons*. The houses here are especially grand as the city has been prosperous since the seventeenth century, the centre of a trade route linking Istanbul to Sinop.

David Walker made his way to the old quarter of Carsi and the leather workers bazaar, where he knew he would be able to pick up a copy of Museum City Safranbolu, with complete listings, maps and historical information, as well as buy clothes and supplies.

Parking up 'Old Faithful', as he now called the car, David Walker and Caviar strolled hand in hand through the bazaar. He held her tightly. He was taking no chances; if she escaped here he might never find her.

They shopped and he bought more clothes for Caviar. They stopped and had a drink outside a pavement café and watched with fascination all the local goings-on. Eventually they jostled their way back to Old Faithful. Consulting his newly acquired map and information, he found out a small pansiyon. It was clean and adequate.

He had a plan.

The final solution.

A challenge.

He picked up the cell phone.

One Hundred and Forty-six

Suicide by cop: he'd read about it somewhere, it was popular in America.

He had decided to die. He knew the game was up, and the only scenario was a gallant death.

A gladiator's death.

Go out in a blaze of glory.

He was going to go out fighting, and he wanted to go out fighting Jack Reec. Two equally matched warriors locked in mortal combat. He hoped they could die together.

Both of them.

One way or another, he was tired of living with the demons in his head. He wanted the peace on the other side, whatever that was. He didn't want to hurt Caviar, but he knew he would if he was alive.

So it was better if he died.

Then she'd be safe.

He made the call.

I answered.

'Hi Jack, it's David. Are you well? It's been a long time.'

'It has,' I answered, a little gobsmacked. 'Where are you?'

'Turkey, Jack,' he told me.

'Big place.'

'You can't imagine.'

'Is Caviar with you?' I asked.

'She is, Jack. Right by my side. Do you want to speak to her?'

'Of course,' I said, thrown off guard.

'I'll put her on.'

'Hi Jack, it's me,' she said sounding cheerful.

'Are you OK?' I asked.

'Sure, Jack, fine. How about you?'

'Worried sick,' I replied. 'Thought you were dead.'

'Fooled you, Jack. It's been a long story, but I'm OK.'

'The whole world thought you were dead for three months. Where have you been?'

David Walker took the phone off her. 'Sorry Jack, time's up.'

'What the fuck are you up to?' I demanded.

'I'll spell it out to you, Jack. If you want her back, come and get her. Winner takes all. I'll be in touch.'

The phone went dead.

One Hundred and Forty-seven

'What's going on, David?' asked Caviar.

'I'll tell you straight,' he said. 'I love you very much, but there is no future for us, or especially me. There's nowhere I can go. I'm an international fugitive, a hunted man, and I want to finish it all. And worse than that, while I'm alive there's the possibility that I might hurt you. I can't let that happen. You've got so much to live for, a massive future.'

'So what are you going to do?' she asked.

'I'm going to go down fighting. Fighting Jack Reec. A sort of duel in the sun.'

'Oh David, don't do it! Please,' she stumbled, starting to cry. 'I can tell them I went willingly with you.' She clutched his hand and sobbed, salty tears streaming down her cheeks. 'Don't

511

do it, it's senseless. I love you.'

'I know,' he sighed emotionally, a misty glaze forming over his eyes. 'But even if you say all that, what about all the soldiers I killed? That won't go away.'

'But...'

'Shush,' he said placing two fingers to her lips.

She fell into his arms and crushed him. She pushed her lips against his with an intensity that she had never felt before. They were both crying now uncontrollably. They began undressing each other slowly and gently until they were both naked on the bed.

They were both fully tanned and immensely fit. It showed in their vigorous lovemaking. Emotionally they rolled from one to another, licking and swallowing each other's tears until there were no more. Neither wanted to climax. They held on until they could hold on no more, then let it go.

The orgasm was the greatest they had ever had. David thrust as deeply as he could into her and she pushed as hard as she could onto him. Crying out, they collapsed, exhausted. They lay there gasping in each other's arms, then slowly relaxed and drifted into a troubled sleep.

One Hundred and Forty-eight

I told the Irishmen, Liam Dooly, Billy Dufacy and Joe Cahill, what David Walker had said.

'So he'll be in touch, will he?' said Dooly, lighting a fag he'd just built up.

'When?' asked Billy Dufacy.

'Didn't say,' I said. 'But we were already going to Turkey anyway.'

'It's a fucking big place,' Dooly grunted, blowing smoke.

'Well, the car's all packed and ready to go,' said Joe Cahill. 'The guns and ammo are stashed in the secret compartment and we're all supplied up. All we need is somewhere to go.'

'Well, Istanbul is as good a place as any,' I

said. 'We'll just have to play it by ear from there.'

'Just let me get my hands on that fucking murdering bastard!' Dooly snarled with snake like venom.

Billy Dufacy started to chuckle, then laugh. Joe Cahill started too. They started me off then. Before long the three of us were in fits. Dooly was looking mad and agitated.

'What's so funny?'

'You, you fucking eejit!' howled Dufacy. 'A murdering bastard, you called him. Hilarious, coming from you!'

We all fell about at that.

'You're all a pack of gobshites,' he chuckled. 'Let's find us a bar and have a fucking hooley.'

One Hundred and Forty-nine

O ld Faithful made it as far as Gerze, and to be fair she was still going strong.

Gerze was one of the prettiest of all the tiny fishing villages along the coast, some forty kilometers from Sinop, and mercifully situated well away from the pitiless roar of the motorway. It has no antiquities or old houses of note, but this calm spot is a genuine haven for true lovers of the sea, though the beach is rather stony. The best places to stay are those situated along the point, where you can sit on a balcony in peace and quiet watching the fishermen harvest *palamut* (a type of mackerel).

This was where David Walker had chosen to spend his last few days with Caviar. He rented a room at a *pansiyon* and they sat that evening listening to the lapping of the waves against the shore and the singing and squawking of seabirds. They held hands and marvelled at the way the bright full moon bathed the point in fluorescent light. They sipped at their glasses of red wine. David Walker smoked a fine cigar. He knew it was bad for his health but he also knew it wouldn't be tobacco that killed him,

Caviar sighed deeply. 'It's so beautiful here, David. Why does it have to end like this?'

'I don't want to talk about it anymore,' he told her. 'It's my fate. Let's enjoy. Let's forget about the rest of the world and give you a few days of life that you can remember forever. And when you're watching TV on death row in some nursing home in your eighties, you can sit there with a smile and remember me.'

Caviar started to have ever such a little cry.

'No more tears. Promise?'

'I promise.'

He raised his glass in a toast. 'To the rest of your life, may it be long and happy.'

'Cheers,' they both said.

'And take no notice of anything you hear me say to Jack Reec. You're going free. When I leave here I won't be coming back. All I ask you to do is stay here a few days until it's over, then call your people and they'll come for you. OK?'

'OK.'

'So let's have some fun.'

One Hundred and Fifty

We weren't far from Istanbul when my cell rang. 'Hello Jack it's me.' 'I've been expecting you,' I growled

'Artvin in five days. Come alone. If you don't, I'll slit her throat. You know I mean it, Jack. I slit your girlfriend's. Artvin.'

'You fucking bastard son of a whore, I'll fucking kill you! You dirty filthy piece of shit, I'll cut your guts out slowly.'

He couldn't hear me. He was gone. I braked the car to a halt and smashed my fists in rage and temper against the steering wheel.

'For fuck's sake, Jack, what's happened?' asked Dooly in a panicky voice. I told him.

Then it all came flooding back, the way he

had slaughtered Barbara like a pig. 'Jack, Jack, calm down! He's trying to get to you. Make you lose your edge.'

'Well he did a fucking good job didn't he?' I cried.

Joe Cahill had the map. He found Artvin. 'Stay cool, auld son. We need to find out all we can about Artvin. We'll get some books in Istanbul. Recce the place.'

'Well, you ain't going in alone,' said Billy Dufacy.

'I have to. If he sees a sign of anyone else he'll slash her up. I know him.'

The three Irishmen exchanged glances. Each one of them knew what they were going to do.'

Liam Dooly tried to lighten things up. 'Sure, that's all of five days away. I say we go into town, get a few reference books, find a hotel and the bar and do some planning over a bottle of Bushmills.'

'Sounds like a plan to me!' howled Billy Dufacy.

So that's what we did, and by the end of the night we had conquered the whole Ottoman Empire.

Pity it wasn't David Walker.

Desmond McGrath

One Hundred and Fifty-one

For the second night in a row, they sat on the balcony overlooking the fishermen on the point. They had eaten locally and drank plenty. They were finishing off the evening with a bottle of red wine.

'So what will you do when you get back?' asked David Walker. 'Recording studios, tours, chat shows. My God, there'll be hundreds of chat shows.'

'No chat shows, no interviews. I'm going home to take some time out,' she said.

'You've had time out,' he told her. 'Nearly four months of it.'

'Yeah, and it's made me realise what a load of bullshit all that superstar stuff is. I don't need that crap any more. I know who I am now.

All this time living with you and nature has taught me something I'll never forget. Money helps, but it's not everything. The important thing is to be at peace with yourself and who you are.'

'I hope it works out for you, Caviar, I really do,' David Walker said with great sincerity.

'If you really mean that, David, can I beg you for the biggest favour in the world?'

'What is it?' he asked hesitantly.

'I know it's a huge thing to ask. I know you want to die, but please don't kill Jack. When you're gone he will be the only friend I'll have left in the world,' she pleaded.

David Walker was silent and thoughtful. A tear welled in his eyes as he gazed at the begging Caviar. He loved her. That's why he wanted to die.

To save her.

He took a long time to answer. 'I'll have to see.'

'Thank you, David,' Caviar sobbed as she grabbed his hand. 'I love you. Thank you.'

One Hundred and Fifty-two

The time had come for the long goodbye. David Walker was heading to the battlefield.

'No tears,' he told her. 'Wait here for three days and then make your call. It will all be over then.'

'How can you just walk into a certain death?' she asked.

'Soldiers do it all the time,' he replied. 'World War One. Why did thousands of men climb out of the trenches to certain death in the face German machine guns? Perhaps death was better than the trenches. Who knows? I don't. Anyway, I don't want to talk about it. You are safe; that's all that matters to me.'

They kissed passionately, then he turned away with a deep breath. He never looked back.

He started Old Faithful and took her out on what must surely be her last journey. She would die too.

In the rusty old boot, under a blanket, were the guns and ammunition he had collected from the dead special forces in spain. A formidable arsenal that included six hand grenades. Very handy tools in an emergency.

He knew that Jack would come alone. He also knew that the Irishmen would follow at a distance. They wouldn't be able to stay away.

Their funeral.

He'd said five days but he was getting there a day early.

For all he knew they were too.

It was a long drive, but as ever Old Faithful was up to the challenge. They didn't build them like that anymore.

Artvin has nothing to recommend it except one decent hotel and some sweeping views, but the surrounding land is beautiful, covered with forests and walnut, apple, cherry and mulberry orchards. Getting to the numerous colourful villages has become almost impossible. There are no tour agents or car rental services.

The country is wild and rugged. Great

ambush country. Trees, rocks, hundred-foot drops, rivers and waterfalls.

Pulling off the dirt road onto a track, David Walker parked Old Faithful for the last time - almost hidden, but still visible to the keen eye.

He climbed around the area selecting his most likely spots for the ambush. He would phone Jack and give him a few clues. Jack should easily find the car. But David Walker wouldn't be there waiting; he was going back a few miles to hide and wait for the Irishmen. They may think they were tough setting off bombs in pubs and shops or using a sniper's rifle from a mile away, but he knew they would be no threat to him.

Lambs to the slaughter.

Then it would be just him and Jack.

Desmond McGrath

One Hundred and Fifty-three

After the latest call from David Walker, we knew we were no more than ten miles away.

'I'm going in alone,' I told them. 'You can get out now.'

'Be reasonable Jack,' pleaded Dooly. 'He's a dangerous man.'

'If he sees you he'll kill her. Now that's final. Get out of the car!' I ordered.

'We'll need our guns, auld son,' said Dooly. 'If he gets you he will be coming for us. I don't intend being the clay pigeon at the shoot.'

'Fair enough,' I said. 'help yourselves.'

'Good luck,' said Billy Dufacy and Joe Cahill.

We all shook hands and the Irishmen took their weapons and a sack of food and drink from the boot of the car. Dooly was building a cigarette. 'Can you leave the car keys under the seat, auld son,' he said lighting up. 'It's a long walk back.'

I got back in the car and started on the last leg of the journey. To what I didn't know. I just hoped there was a better outcome than the last time we met.

'He's a fucking eejit,' snarled Dooly. 'The girl's probably already dead. He's not going to bring her out here to get in his way in a firefight.'

'I was thinking that,' said Joe Cahill. 'Unless he has her tied up and stashed somewhere.'

'And where does that get her if Jack kills Walker? Is he going to give him a letter telling where she is? I don't fucking think so!' scoffed Billy Dufacy.

'So what do we do, Liam?' asked Cahill.

'We find a bit of shade, have a bite to eat and a swig of the good stuff, and we follow him.'

'He won't like it,' said Dufacy

'Tough shit on him, then,' said Dooly, taking a drag.

One Hundred and Fifty-four

D avid Walker was carrying a sack with three AK47 assault rifles in it and four Spanish hand grenades. He had enough food and drink for a day and was making good headway in cover well away from the track. Every now and then he would sneak up to the road and take a look.

Nothing.

He backtracked to cover and carried on. His finely tuned senses detected a faint smell of smoke. He had travelled at least five miles. He took cover behind a large tree. He hid a rifle behind a rock, then another one behind a tree some distance away.

One of the Irishmen was well in front smoking a roll-up. The two behind were stupidly walking together, actually bumping

into each other on the uneven ground. He crept
to another large tree and stood behind it. He let
the point man pass, and as the other two
walked past the tree he moved quietly around it
until he was behind it. When they were six
paces ahead he stepped out.

'I say, old chaps. Anyone for cricket?' he
said. Dufacy and Cahill turned in shock.

'Catch!' called David Walker and threw them
the grenade.

Joe Cahill instinctively caught it. For a split
second of horror before it exploded, he realised
what it was. It blasted his head straight off his
body, along with his arms. It also ripped a hole
into his chest. Billy Dufacy was peppered with
shrapnel. The blast threw him to the ground.
The molten metal that ripped through this
throat, severing his carotid artery, killed him.

Liam Dooly was on the ground. David Walker
was behind the tree. Dooly was in shock. He
could see the two bodies but had no idea what
had happened. He was sweating.

Profusely.

He was a hardened killer but he still knew
fear. It was one thing killing people, it was
another being killed. He felt fucked. He was
lying on the ground in the open with nowhere to
go.

David Walker was a sport. 'I presume that's you, Dooly - the feared and dangerous IRA assassin, murderer of women and children. How do you want it? A fair fight in the open or a grenade on the ground? Your choice. Its of little consequence to me.'

Dooly was trapped. He was starting to panic. 'You think you're so fucking brave slashing young girls' throats!' he called out.

'Touche,' conceded David Walker. 'So how's it to be? I'm getting hungry.'

'Guns.'

'OK. Stand up and I'll step out. Then on the count of three.'

'This ain't a fucking cowboy film.'

'I'm giving you a chance. Take it or leave it.'

'Fuck you, then,' Dooley said and stood up.

David Walker popped from behind the tree and lobbed the grenade at Dooley's feet. He just had time to scream, 'You double-crossing bastard!' before it went off.

'That's for Birmingham,' David Walker snarled.

Desmond McGrath

One Hundred and Fifty-five

I saw the car and braked to a stop. I was tense and nervous. I was a sitting duck. There were trees and rocks everywhere. I cautiously scouted the area. I couldn't sense or feel David Walker. Something told me that he wasn't close. I followed my instincts and thoroughly reconnoitred the area.

There was loads of cover and hiding places. If it wasn't by chance then he'd chosen the battleground well. About a quarter of a mile ahead I realised we were on a plateau. There was a sheer drop of a hundred feet to a rocky bottom with a few trees and bushes.

No escape that way.

It was now about two in the afternoon and very hot. I sat in the shade of a tree. I wasn't as physically fit as I should be. The easy life had softened me up. I certainly wasn't fighting fit. And then I saw it.

A white rag on the end of a stick waving above a rock.

'Truce, Jack?' I heard David Walker call. I recognised his voice.

Was it a trick?

'Why not?' I called. 'It's a bit too hot to be running around shooting.'

'My feelings exactly,' he called back. 'I've already had one skirmish. Could do with a break. I've got a bottle if you fancy a drink.'

'Bring it over,' I just couldn't help but admire his nerve. 'It's not a trick, is it?' I asked.

'Jack, you must know. You're not stupid. If I'd wanted to I would have taken you out by now. You've lost your edge. I could have shot you to pieces any time I liked.'

Of course I knew he was right. He emerged from behind the rock and threw away the flag. He sauntered over carrying a bag. Christ, I thought, he looks lean and fit.

'We meet again,' He smiled.

'You don't mind if we don't shake hands,' I

said.

'Boxers touch gloves.'

'We're not boxing.'

'Just boxing clever. Mind if I sit?'

'Free country.'

He passed me a bottle of red wine with a screw top.

'I've got two,' he said producing another.

'We unscrewed the tops and threw them away. We wouldn't be needing them. After a long welcome swig I said, 'You mentioned a skirmish.'

'So I did, yes,' he replied. 'The three Irishmen, the ones you said you weren't bringing.'

'I told them not to follow me,' I was almost apologising.

'Well, I'm sure they're very sorry. They're dead,' he said almost matter-of-factly.

I was shocked but didn't know what to say.

'Don't be mad, Jack,' he said. 'There were three of them armed and dangerous. And they were all killers, and you know what they say about living and dying by the sword.'

I knew. 'Where's Caviar?'

'She's safe and well, Jack. She's a great kid. We've had a really fun time. She's free as a bird, but I've asked her to wait a few days to call her people to give us time to finish our unfinished business.'

He took another drink.

'What's all this about?' I asked. 'I just don't understand.'

He sighed deeply. 'Jack, I don't understand it myself. I'm fucked up badly in the head. I'm schizophrenic, mentally ill. I told Caviar to go because the other side of me might emerge one day and hurt her. I couldn't stand that.'

'Get help,' I told him.

'It's too late for that, Jack. I've done too many bad things. And I want to say now that I'm sorry about your Barbara. That wasn't me; it was the other bloke, the one in my head. The real me would never have harmed a hair of her head. She was lovely. I'm sorry.'

I was choking back my emotions.

'Have another drink, Jack. It helps,' he said sympathetically.

I did.

'So how does this end?' I asked. 'I don't get it.'

'I'm here to die Jack. I'm tired of living like this. I don't want to kill any more innocent people. The original plan was for me to prove I am the better man, and that we kill each other in a firefight - which by the way Jack, I already have. I could easily have killed you. So that bit's settled.'

'So?'

'So let us have a good drink and some food, get a good night's sleep and in the morning take up positions and shoot it out like soldiers. You see, Jack, I haven't got the balls to kill myself. I need you to do it for me.'

'So be it,' I said.

Desmond McGrath

One Hundred and Fifty-six

'**S**o this is it, Jack,' said David Walker. 'For whatever happens next, thank Caviar.'

'I don't understand.'

'You will. Trust me.'

'This is bizarre.'

'I'll start in the trees. Where do you want to start?'

David Walker had an AK47. I had a MAC-10 machine pistol. I was worried. I wasn't psyched up for this. It just seemed so surreal, like an out-of-body experience. But I suddenly realised that this was for real and that I'd better get my act together.

'The rocks.'

'Then let's do it.'

We ran to our positions and dived for cover. I poked my head around the rock and a bullet slammed a chunk out of it. I ducked back in.

This was fucking madness. I couldn't believe it was happening. David Walker ran from cover to another tree. I fired a few rounds but too late. He charged again throwing himself to the ground and rolling to another tree.

Christ, he was fit and fast. I tried another peek and realised he had me covered as another round crashed into the rock. I was trapped. I was thinking fast now. The only way I could go was back, using the rock as cover. Crawling on my belly as fast as I could, I got to another rock behind me. I didn't think he could have seen me.

If I could get to the next rock to my left unseen I might be able to outflank him and get behind him. But what was he going to be doing?

Then a thought occurred to me. If he was telling the truth about Caviar, then what was I doing here? If I could get to the car I could just fuck off out of it.

But I couldn't bear the thought of him calling me a coward. I pulled myself together and got crawling. From rock to rock I was making progress down the left flank.

Then I ran out of rocks.

There was a hundred-yard stretch of open ground to the trees. My eyes searched everywhere for a sign of David Walker. I had to cover that open ground. I tried to figure out if I should crawl or run. If he saw me and I was crawling I was dead. If he didn't see me it was safer. But if I ran for it there was a far greater chance of being seen.

Decision time.

I got to my feet and charged. Halfway across, bullets ripped up the ground around. Jesus Christ, I don't need this, I thought. At the last ten feet I threw myself in the trees. Gasping for breath and pouring sweat, I lay on my back, panting.

'Well done, Jack! I bet that knackered you a bit,' David Walker called. Then he laughed. 'Take a break. I can wait.'

He was laughing at me. Taking the piss. I was getting angry. 'Fuck you, Walker,' I shouted back.

'Language Jack.'

I was getting back my breath. I decided to take the fight to him. With a quick burst from the MAC-10, I charged forward from tree to tree. I could see him ahead retreating deeper into the wood. He stopped and turned for a second and fired off a few rounds that stripped bark from the trees around me. Then he ran on again.

I remembered then about the hundred-foot drop ahead. No escape here, I'd thought when I saw it before. I pressed on with more enthusiasm. Did he know about the drop?

David Walker knew about it all right, and he also knew about the hollow in the ground big enough to hide him. He'd also earlier cut down a bush and left it next to it. He jumped in and pulled the bush over it.and waited.

The trees ended fifty yards from the drop; it was open ground and no sign of David Walker. He couldn't have doubled back. I'd have seen him. Shit! I didn't know what to do. I saw a bush about halfway over the ground and decided to crawl behind it. Slithering quickly I got to it. There was no sign of David Walker anywhere. Perhaps he was climbing down the rock face... I hadn't inspected it to see how difficult it would be to someone who could climb. I crawled around the bush towards the edge.

'Jack you're crap.'

I froze.

'Don't move, and throw aside the MAC. How did you ever get into special forces?'

'It was a long time ago,' I replied. I rolled over and sat up. David Walker was leaning on the edge of the hollow aiming the AK straight at me. 'So what now?'

'Well, I suppose I've got to kill you,' he said matter-of-factly. 'I'm sure you wouldn't want it any other way in the circumstances.'

'Well, actually...' I began.

'Just kidding,' he laughed.

'Look, if you're going to do it just do it,' I said. 'I'm tired of all these games.'

'Well, actually Jack, I'm not,' he said. 'And do you want to know the only reason why? Because Caviar begged me not to. She said that with me gone you would be the only friend she had left in the world. She cried and begged for your life, Jack. She even thanked me in advance. How could I betray her?'

He threw down the AK.

'Now do the decent thing Jack and empty that MAC into my heart.'

I stood up and picked up the MAC-10. It was still almost fully loaded. I aimed it at David Walker's torso. But I just couldn't pull the trigger.

My nerve was gone.

'Do it, for fuck's sake. Help me, Jack.'

My hands started to tremble. The gun was shaking. I'd lost whatever it took to kill a man in cold blood.

'You're a useless piece of shit, Jack. Tell Caviar I love her.'

Then he charged past me and launched himself into the air down the cliff.

I couldn't bring myself to look over. I threw the MAC-10 to the ground and walked away.

He was right.

I was a useless piece of shit.

And I felt it.

One Hundred and Fifty-seven

Peter Philips sat at his desk on *Sky News*. 'The most sensational story of the century! Missing rock icon Caviar has been found alive and well. Rumours abound, but with as yet no press release all we know is that she has been found in a small fishing village in Turkey: Gerze. Emma Griffiths is there now with a live report. Over to you, Emma. What can you tell us?'

'Yes, Peter, this is indeed sensational news. Caviar has not been seen, but apparently after a phone call to her manager a helicopter is being sent to collect her. Local police have interviewed her and are satisfied that no crime has been committed in Turkey. However, there is an immigration issue regarding possible illegal entry. How she got here is still a mystery.

'The whole incident is shrouded in secrecy. Caviar has refused to speak or give an interview. Locals say she arrived with a man. A handsome, well-spoken man by all accounts, in his mid-thirties. They arrived about a week ago but he has not been seen for the last three days.

'Wait a minute, Peter, the media scrum is on. A helicopter is landing. A young woman with a coat over her head, who I can only assume is Caviar, is running to it followed by four men. They're not hanging around, Peter. They're taking off. They're gone. The plot thickens. What more can I say? This is Emma Griffiths handing you back to *Sky News* studios.'

One Hundred and Fifty-eight

When I got back to the car I was shaking. Dooly's bottle of Bushmills was on the back seat. It was half full. When I finished drinking it was a quarter full.

It was then I remembered Dooly, Dufacy and Cahill. Where were they? I knew they were dead. But what should I do about it?

I made a quick decision.

Forget about them and get out of Turkey as fast as possible. There was nothing I could do for them and no way was I involving the Turkish Police. The bodies might not be found for months, and as they weren't Turkish I doubted that the police would even bother about them. They wouldn't waste the money. I certainly wasn't about to kick over a can of worms. I had another slug of whiskey and stopped shaking.

549

I was starting to think more clearly now. There was no way I was driving all the way back across Europe on my own to get back to Spain. I would dump the car and take a plane from Istanbul.

There was spare ammo and a couple of handguns in the secret compartment. I dumped them. I cleared the car of anything that had any sort of ID. I checked the number plates. They were stuck on. Good. I could pull them off easily.

My plan was to get to Istanbul Airport, park the car, tear off the plates and dump them. Then buy a ticket to anywhere in Spain, or anywhere closer if needs be. I just knew I had to get out of Turkey.

Quick.

I had one last slug of Bushmills and tossed the bottle. I turned the car around and started the return journey. I hoped it was true what David Walker had said. that Caviar was safe. I switched on the radio for company; all I could get was Turkish music. To be honest it was alright.

I knew I had a long drive so I just got down to it. It was now that the full impact of the loss of my friends set in.

I felt something between loneliness, sorrow

and guilt. I told myself that I had got them into it. Then I said no, I told them not to follow me. They only had themselves to blame.

It didn't work.

They were coming to help me. That was the truth.

Maybe it was the Irish whiskey but it kept ringing in my ears.

'You're a useless piece of shit, Jack.'

I drove on. And on.

I stopped for fuel and drove on. It was dark now and I was tired. But I just drove on and on.

It was after midnight when I started to pick up the signs for Istanbul. At 2.00 a.m. I saw the best sign of all.

An aeroplane.

I followed the signs to the airport, parked the car and tore off the plates. I lost them in a trash bin.

Passport in hand, I strode through the airport and was lucky enough to get a ticket to Madrid for the morning. I found myself a comfortable seat in the loungeand fell asleep.

I woke early and freshened up in the toilets. I

still looked rough. The flight was an early one and on time. I went through to Departures, had some food and a beer and boarded.

I was on my way home.

One Hundred and Fifty-nine

Caviar would speak to noone. No press, no TV, no interviews of any description.

She flew first class to New York. Then first class to Tampa. A Lincoln Town Car collected her at the airport and drove her the hundred miles to Spring Hill where she had a home.

She was happy in Florida. She loved Spring Hill.

People gave her space and left her alone. She didn't even look like Caviar any more after her months in the wilds. She told the driver to stop at the mall and she went in shopping. A couple of people took a second look but decided it couldn't be. She bought basic food provisions and wine and beer and a bottle of vodka and wheeled her brown bags to the town car. The driver jumped out and opened the trunk for her.

Together they loaded it in.

'Thanks, José,' she told the Hispanic driver.

'You're welcome Ma'am,' he replied. 'Home now?'

She thought for a second. 'Na,' she said. 'Take me to Sam's Bar.'

Sam's Bar was fifteen minutes away at Hudson Beach. It was a popular bar with a large outside terrace. There was a four-piece rock band playing. They were pretty good. The lead singer, she thought, was great.

'Come on, José,' she said. 'Take a break. Have a beer.'

'I'm driving Man.'

'One Bud ain't gonna do any damage. Let's find a table.'

'But Ma'am.'

'José, it's an order. OK?' Caviar laughed. 'I'm not sitting here on my own. I might get picked up!'

The cocktail waitress took their order. Caviar had a mai tai. They settled back and listened as the band played Foreigner. Caviar applauded.

She ordered another mai tai and a mineral

water for Jose. The band played Bon Jovi. They were great and Caviar was loving it. Two more Mai Tais and she was on her feet, rocking. The lead singer noticed her. She looked vaguely familiar.

He finished the song and thanked the audience.

'Hey, lady,' he spoke into the mike to Caviar. 'Do I know you?'

All eyes turned to Caviar.

'I get around a lot.'

'You look familiar.'

'I cut a record once.'

'You wanna sing it?'

'You wouldn't know it. Do you know any of that Caviar's stuff? I can do her.'

'Who doesn't? You wanna come up?'

'Why the hell not? I'm drunk.'

The audience howled with laughter. Caviar threaded her way through the tables onto the stage.'

'I think I need another mai tai,' she said into the mic.

'On me,' shouted a man from the audience.

'Thank you.'

In denim shorts and vest she turned and consulted with the band. They fixed a set and the band let rip. Caviar burst into the first song and the crowd were on their feet. She sang six more and they went crazy.

She tried to get offstage.

'More, more, more!' they chanted.

'What the heck. Get me another mai tai.'

A quick consultation with the band and the encore was set.

They never had a night out like that in Sam's Bar before and never would again.

Caviar thanked the band and kissed them one by one.

'You were great, guys.'

'You too. Who are you?'

'I busk for a living.'

José took her home.

He was the only person there who knew who she was. What a story to tell the grandkids!

'She even *looks* like Caviar,' someone said.

One Hundred and Sixty

From Madrid I took a flight to Malaga and a taxi to the farm.

I've never in my life been so relieved to be home. I switched on all the outside lights and pulled a bottle of cava from the fridge. Bringing a glass, I flopped into my favourite chair by the pool.

Home sweet home.

I drank the first glass too quickly and the bubbles made me choke. I poured a second glass and began to feel calmer.

I was worn out. David Walker was right. 'You're crap, Jack,' he said. Well, I'd made my mind up. This was it. No more diving, no more trying to be a hero. I was back in the sanctuary of my farm and I wasn't setting foot off it until I felt ready.

I was emotionally and physically fucked. I'd lost another friend, Dooly, but he knew the score. The other two were just foot soldiers. They knew the score too. They underestimated David Walker. A fatal mistake. I thought I could match him but never really had a chance.

He could have taken me any time. I was lucky to be alive. And now I quit, I quit the world. I just wanted some solitude.

Some space

My phone rang. It was Caviar.

'What happened, Jack?'

I told her.

'The last words he said were, "Tell Caviar I love her."'

'Thanks, Jack.'

She cut me off.

Tanned, but a white man.

It spooked him a bit.

All on his own out here with a dead body.

He got as close as he dared.

Then the body groaned.

So quietly it was almost inaudible.

Frightened out of his wits, the little peasant boy ran off, rabbits dancing all around his legs.

'Papa, Papa!' he shouted frantically. 'Papa, Papa!'

The End

Epilogue

The little peasant boy had been hunting all day. He was no more than ten or eleven. There was a string of ten rabbits tied around his waist. He hunted the same trails every day.

He was making his way along the bottom of the rock face when he saw something that he knew wasn't there yesterday. He couldn't make out what it was from this distance, but it was under one of only half a dozen trees by the rock face.

Cautiously he crept towards it. As he got closer he saw that it was the lifeless body of David Walker. He'd never seen a dead body before and it scared him, but he still went right up close. Should he prod it? He didn't know. The body wasn't local. The man looked more Northern European.

I made her wait a minute. I spoke again.

'Only if they can come too.'

She was sobbing on the end of the phone.

'Make it quick, Jack.'

cooking. The girls were giggling and laughing as usual, glasses in hand.

There had been a short shower earlier that heightened the aromas of the garden. The orange and lemon smelled stronger than usual, but my favourite was always the damp earth.

I loved it. I could inhale it forever.

'Come on, you pair,' I said. 'I don't mind cooking it but I'm not a waiter.

'Ooh,' they said, 'Mr Bossy!'

They'd had enough.

The phone rang.

It was Caviar. In Florida

'I'm back, Jack,' she said. 'I really need you. Can you come?'

'Don't know,' I said. 'I'll have to ask my friends.'

'Who's that?'

'Horny and Delicious.'

'They're there!' she cried.

'They are. I'll ask them.'

She arrived back in Spring Hill even browner than when she left. But refreshed, invigorated, ready to conquer the world again. Not that she needed to. Since her disappearance over six months ago now, she had sold more records than she ever had before.

Everything she had ever done was re-released and went straight to the top of the charts. The money was rolling in faster than a runaway bobsleigh.

But she needed her friends.

I'd spent the last three months at the farm.

Never left it once.

Anything I wanted I had it delivered.

Which reminds me: Horny Formore and Delicious Fantastico.

Horny took it bad at first about Dooly. But she was strong and resourceful. She got over it. They were practically living at the farm, and it was no hardship for me, I can tell you.

Swimsuits were banned as always and we all had beautiful all-over tans. Time is a great healer, and the long summer days and nights helped. Not to mention great food and drink.

It was almost midnight and I was still

One Hundred and Sixty-two

Three Months Later.

Caviar had gone off the radar.

In her quest for peace, she'd taken the Winnebago across America and found solitude in the mountains of Idaho, Nevada, Montana, Wyoming, Utah and Colorado.

With a population of only 975,000, Montana was her favourite state. Second came Wyoming with a population of only 544,000.

She had found herself.

She had finally come to terms with the fact that her friend, lover, soul-mate and kidnapper, David Walker, was dead.

It was time to rejoin the world.